The Pastor's Son

WILLIAM W. WALTER

The Pastor's Son

William W. Walter

© 1st World Library – Literary Society, 2004
PO Box 2211
Fairfield, IA 52556
www.1stworldlibrary.org
First Edition

LCCN: 2004091288

Softcover ISBN: 1-59540-699-9
eBook ISBN: 1-59540-799-5

Purchase *"The Pastor's Son"*
as a traditional bound book at:
www.1stWorldLibrary.org/purchase.asp?ISBN=1-59540-699-9

1st World Library Literary Society is a nonprofit organization dedicated to promoting literacy by:

- Creating a free internet library accessible from any computer worldwide.
- Hosting writing competitions and offering book publishing scholarships.

Readers interested in supporting literacy through sponsorship, donations or membership please contact:
literacy@1stworldlibrary.org
Check us out at: www.1stworldlibrary.org

The Pastor's Son

contributed by the Charles Family
in support of
1st World Library Literary Society

DEDICATED TO

F. S. B.
IN GRATEFUL RECOGNITION
OF WORK WELL DONE

CONTENTS

PREFACE

My sole reason for writing this book and placing it before the public is to call the public's attention to *another book*, wherein is contained the Christ truth, the understanding of which will free you from all your troubles.

If in sin, it shows the way out; if sick, it will heal you; if grief-stricken, it will mend your broken heart; if in poverty, it will give you plenty. I speak from experience, having been sick for more than seven years, at the edge of the grave, reduced to poverty, and all earthly hope gone. I was rescued from this inferno on earth, my health restored, my supply sufficient, my joy complete; surely I can say, my cup of happiness runneth over. Truly that book sayeth - "Come all ye that are heavy laden and I will give you rest."

CHAPTER I

THANKSGIVING MORNING

"What a beautiful Thanksgiving morning this is," said the Rev. James A. Williams to his son Walter, as he looked out of the dining-room window. "There isn't a cloud in the sky, and this soft, balmy breeze from the south makes one almost believe that it is a June morning instead of the 30th of November. I know there will be a large attendance at church this morning, which will please me very much, as I have prepared an excellent sermon, and feel certain that the congregation will enjoy it."

He glanced at his son as he finished speaking, and some of the joy and cheerfulness that had shown in his eyes faded away, for he saw no return of his joy and happiness on his child's face; all that was written there was sorrow, pain, and feebleness.

His son, who was nearly seventeen, had always been sickly and feeble since birth; the best physicians had been employed, change of climate had been tried, and everything else that promised relief, but of no avail. The best specialists had been consulted, but they gave little hope that hereditary consumption could be cured, for the minister's wife had been similarly afflicted for many years.

The Rev. Williams thought silently for a few moments, then tried to regain his cheerfulness by changing the subject to something that might interest his son; so he said, "Well, wife, I suppose that turkey Deacon Phillips gave us will be done to perfection by dinner time; I am beginning to feel hungry already, just from thinking of it and it is two hours to dinner time yet."

Lillian his wife, looked up from her work with a careworn expression on her face, and said, "Yes, it is a fine large turkey." His wife always looked worn-out and tired, for not being strong and still compelled to do all the housework, it fatigued her very much.

It had not always been this way, for the Rev. Williams was a man of ability, his congregation large, and his salary ample under ordinary circumstances, but the constant drain of physicians' bills, and the great expense of sending mother and son to a warm climate each fall, as the rigors of the northern winters were considered too hard for the two invalids to bear, had reduced them almost to poverty; consequently the expense of a maidservant had long since been dispensed with.

Rev. Williams now turned to go to his study, and as he was turning, said, "I know that I will do justice to that turkey, after delivering my long sermon, and I am very thankful to Deacon Phillips, and to God, for having given it to us."

There was silence for a few moments after the father left the room; then Mrs. Williams said: "Walter, dear, you had better get ready for church; I will soon have this turkey so I can leave it, then I will get ready and we will both go to church, there to give thanks to God."

Walter turned to his mother saying, "What have we to be thankful for, mother?"

His mother looked up, somewhat startled, and answered, "Why for everything that God gave us." "Everything, mother?" asked Walter.

"Yes dear, everything."

"Oh, mother, I don't see how I am going to do that, father told me that God gave me this sickness, and I don't see how I can feel thankful to Him for making me suffer."

The mother anxiously looked at her son, then said, "Remember Walter, Jesus Christ, the only Son of God, also suffered."

"Yes, I know, but it was not God that made Him suffer, it was the Pharisees; but father said it was God gave me this sickness and that I must bear it with love and patience, which I have tried to do, but I have never been able to understand why a good and loving God should care to see me suffer."

"I am sure I cannot tell," said his mother, "but it must be for some good purpose; we will ask your father to explain some time. Now hurry and get ready."

A few minutes later they both walked to the church, which was only a short distance away, and entered its wide-open doors.

CHAPTER II

THE TURKEY DINNER

"Well wife, what did you think of my sermon?" asked the pastor as he sat down to enjoy the turkey dinner.

"I think it was the best sermon you ever delivered, James," answered his wife, quietly.

"I think so, too," said James, "and what's more, it ought to make every person that heard it feel very thankful to God, for all He has given them," then looking around the room he asked, "Where is Walter?"

"I don't know," said his wife, "he became so nervous and tired, that he left just before the last hymn was sung. I suppose he went up to his room, you had better call him to dinner."

"I will," answered the pastor, and going to the hall door, he called aloud, "Walter, dinner is ready."

"All right father, I will be down in a minute," came back the answer in a rather faint voice. The pastor turned to his wife and asked, "Do you think that last medicine is doing him any more good than the others we have tried?"

His wife raised her sad face to his, and replied, "No, James, I don't think it is helping him, for he seems to get weaker and more nervous all the time. I feel that he is losing ground even more rapidly than I am."

Here Walter entered the room, his face more flushed than usual, and his father's watchful eye took note of it, but he spoke up cheerfully, "Just look at that turkey, Walter, isn't it a fine one? See how nice and evenly it is browned, and the oyster dressing, I'll bet it's fit for a king."

Walter merely glanced at the turkey, then seated himself beside his mother.

After the pastor had said grace, he picked up the carving knife and said, "Now, son, just tell me what piece you like best and I will have it carved out for you before you can say, Jack Robinson."

"You are very kind, father, but I don't believe I care for any turkey, I am not feeling very well," answered Walter.

"Just try a little, Walter," said the mother coaxingly, "I know it must be very tender and nice, for Deacon Phillips said it was a young turkey."

"Yes, Walter," said his father, "hand me your plate, and I will give you a little of the dark and a little of the light meat, with some of this delicious dressing."

The boy listlessly handed over his plate without any more ado, his father put onto it a liberal piece of each kind of meat and some dressing, then handed it back, with the remark, "Eat all you can son, for it will make you strong." Then he added, "Now wife, it's your turn, I know you like the dark meat the best," and while he was talking he carved a nice piece of the turkey and laid it on her plate, and then said, "Now father, it is your turn, and I know your failing to be the leg," and suiting the action to the word, he carved for himself the leg.

Then, addressing his son once more, he asked, "How did you like the sermon, Walter?"

"I thought it was very fine, father, and as I looked over the congregation, I could see many heads nodding their approval of your words telling them they ought to be thankful, and I tried, oh, so hard, to be thankful, but I couldn't, for something seemed to say, you have nothing to be thankful for, God gave you this sickness as a punishment. I tried to think what I had done to merit this punishment, but found it could not have been anything I had done, as I remembered that you had said I always had been sick even when a little child, and then - "

"Tut, tut, child, now don't get excited," said the pastor. "We all know that your punishment is not for anything you may have done, but you are probably suffering for the sins of others, the same as Jesus did; why, Walter, just think, Jesus Christ died for all our sins."

"For my sins, father?" asked the boy.

"Yes, Walter, all our sins."

"But father, I don't see how that could be. We weren't any of us living at that time, and if we sinned, it must have been since then, and Jesus could not die for sins that had not been committed."

The father was so surprised at what he heard, that for a moment he just stared at his son; the idea was entirely new to him, and yet it was only common sense. He tried to find some reply that would be reasonable, but before he found it, the boy continued.

"I cannot believe that God punishes any one person for the sins of another. If He would do this, He would not be a just God. Why, father, even man is more just than that. Supposing Judge Baxter had pronounced sentence like this: 'Yes, I find Mose Webster guilty of stealing Mr. Johnson's chickens, and have decided to send the Rev. James Williams to the county jail for ten months, because Mose Webster stole those chickens,' would you think that justice? and could you feel thankful to the judge for sending you to jail to suffer in the place of Mose Webster, and - "

"Silence, child," said the father, more sternly than he had ever spoken to his son before. He was so confused by what the boy had said that he could not find words to speak. After a time he said, "Walter, never let me hear you say anything like that again, to think that you, a minister's son, should say such things. Why, they are almost blasphemous."

"Never mind, James," said the mother; "think how hard it must be to suffer year in and year out, without any relief, and remember, dear, that even some of the apostles doubted at times. Now, let us finish our dinner." Then, turning to her son, she added, "father will explain all this to you as soon as he finds time."

The father looked at the flushed face of the boy and his

anger softened, then in a kind voice said: "I think it would be a very nice idea for us to set aside one or two evenings each week for Bible reading and study; in this way we would all get a better understanding of God, and His great love for mankind. What do you think of that plan, Walter?"

"I should enjoy it, as there is a great deal in the Bible that I should like to have explained."

"All right, Walter, now what would you say to starting our Bible class to-morrow evening?"

"That would please me," said Walter.

"How about you, mother?" asked the pastor.

"Oh, I certainly want to be a member of the class. I know it will be very entertaining and instructive, besides it will be such a pleasant way to spend the long winter evenings."

"Why mother, I thought we were going south this winter."

"No, child, it will be impossible for us to go this year. You know that this last medicine which you and I are taking costs father five dollars per bottle, and we each need a bottle a week, so it has been impossible for father to save the money necessary for our going."

For a moment the boy's face looked sad and grave, and the pastor swallowed a lump that had risen in his throat, for it hurt the good man severely to think that he had not the necessary funds to gratify their every wish, but had already borrowed more than he could pay back in several years. Still he was willing to make more sacrifices, had his wife agreed, but she had said on one occasion when they were discussing this subject, "No, James, I will not leave you again. I think the separation does us as much harm as the warm climate does good, and I feel that we have not many more years to be together, so I cannot bear the thought of being separated from you for another five months. I think Walter and I will be better off to be at home with you. We need not go out in the cold very much, and you and I can arrange some way to entertain and amuse Walter."

The pastor had answered: "Well, Lillian, it may be the better way, for I must confess that these long separations were very unpleasant to me, yet I was more than willing to endure them, if thereby you and Walter could be benefited, still it seems that the change of climate idea did not prove as beneficial as we had hoped for, but please don't speak in that hopeless strain again, for you certainly have heard that old saying, 'while there is life there is hope,' so never give up, and remember that there are many noted physicians and chemists, working day and night to get a sure cure for tuberculosis, and who knows but that the morrow will bring it forth. You know that I am constantly on the lookout for everything that looks promising."

And so the thought of a southern trip had been dismissed.

CHAPTER III

WHAT WALTER FOUND

Dinner over, they all arose from their seats at the table, and the father asked, "Walter, what part of the Bible shall we start to study first?"

"I hardly know, father," said Walter.

"Well, you can take the old family Bible, look it over and then decide. As for myself I have very little choice; I have read and studied it so often that I feel very familiar with all it contains."

"All right; father, may I go up to my room now?"

"Yes, certainly, if you choose, but I should think you would rather be outside to-day, it is so warm, and there won't be many more days like this this year."

"I believe I would rather go to my room," said the boy, starting in that direction.

"Just as you please, son," said the father, as he stepped through the hall to enter the library. Walter went quickly up stairs to his room, and his mother wondered greatly at his hurry.

Once in his room he closed the door and quietly locked it, then going to his trunk, he excitedly pulled forth a little book with a black leather cover which looked very much like a small Bible. He opened it and began reading in a low tone. "*Science and Health, with Key to the Scriptures, by Mary Baker G. Eddy.*" "Yes, I am sure it is the same book that lovely lady down south told me about, and asked mother to get me one, but mother had said, 'no, we will never try Christian Science; we are real Christians and believe in God.' I could not hear everything they said, but I did hear the lady say, 'I don't see how you can say that you believe that God is all Good, and at the same time think He made your lovely boy sick.' I did not hear mother's reply, but I know she was angry. Now I wonder who lost this book? I saw no one in sight when I picked it up this morning; there is no name in it, so I can't return it to the owner. I wonder if I ought to read it? I don't need to believe it if I do read it. Anyway, that lady did not look like a person that was bad, and she said she read Science and Health every day, and that it had healed her of a severe sickness."

As he talked he turned a few pages and then read, "Contents, Chapter I, Prayer. I wonder if that chapter is in favor of prayer or against it. I suppose though it must be against it by the way mother acted towards that lady." He laid his head upon his hands and thought silently for some time, then raised his head and said, "Well, I am going to read it. That lady said reading 'Science and Health' cured her, and I am going to see if it will cure me if I read it. I suppose the place to start is Chapter I."

Walter began to read to himself: "Science and Health. Chapter I, Prayer.

"For verily I say unto you, that whosoever shall say unto this mountain, be thou removed, and be thou cast into the sea, and shall not doubt in his heart, but shall believe that those things which he saith shall come to pass, he shall have whatsoever he saith. Therefore I say unto you, what things whatsoever ye desire when ye pray, believe that ye receive them, and ye shall have them. Your Father knoweth what things ye have need of before ye ask him. Christ Jesus."

Then he stopped and said, "Why that is just the same as I read in our Bible; there certainly can be no bad in that. But maybe they only printed that so as to ridicule it farther on in the book; anyway, I wonder what Jesus Christ meant, when he said, '*therefore I say unto you, what things whatsoever ye desire when ye pray, believe ye shall receive them and ye shall have them.*' Oh, how often and how earnestly have I prayed for health, with tears running down my cheeks, but my prayers never seem to have been answered; now I wonder why, for I know that what Jesus Christ said must be true, for He was the Son of God, and would not deceive us; why, oh why, doesn't God answer my prayers?"

He stopped to consider for a moment, then turned pale as death, pressed his thin hands to his breast, as a new thought came to his consciousness, then he gasped in a whisper, "I - believe - I - know." He paused a moment, then continued, "It must be that - I see it all now; I see my mistake. I prayed to God for health, and in the next instant doubted Him, doubted that He would heal me. In fact, I never really believed that He would heal me, and Jesus said, 'Believe that ye receive.' Oh, can this really be true. I am so excited I can hardly think. Here I am again, this time doubting the word of Christ." Then he jumped up with the exclamation, "I must tell

William W. Walter

father, for his prayers are not answered, and it must be for the same reason. No, I don't mean that. My father is a minister and he could not doubt God. But why aren't his prayers answered? I don't know what to do. If I tell father or mother, they may take the book away, and then my last hope would be gone. I think I will read it first." So saying, he sat down in an easy rocker, and was soon absorbed in what he was reading, nor did he notice how the time flew until he heard his mother's anxious voice and knock at the door.

He answered at once, and hastily put the book back in his trunk, then went to the door and opened it.

His mother greeted him with, "Why, Walter, what is the matter? Since when have you taken to locking your door in the daytime? You look so flushed and excited, and we haven't heard a sound from you all the afternoon. We were beginning to get alarmed about you, so I came up to see what was the matter, and to tell you that supper was ready. What have you been doing? Don't you feel as well as usual? Tell me, Walter, are you worse?"

"No, mother, I am not worse, I only became so absorbed in reading that I forgot all about time, and also that I had locked the door."

His mother did not think to ask him what he was reading, as she had always been very careful to see that no reading matter that was at all questionable was brought into the house, so she had no idea that he had been reading anything but what she had read and deemed proper.

"We had better hurry down, Walter, as father is

waiting for his supper."

They both started down the stairs, his mother still talking to him; but he scarcely heard a word she said, for his thoughts were still centered on what he had read. And now that his excitement had abated, there seemed to be a hopeful gleam in his eyes. As soon as they entered the room, his father noticed that his eyes were brighter, but took it as a bad sign.

All through the evening meal they had to address him several times before he would answer, and his father's heart grew heavy as he noticed the thoughtful mood of his son.

When they had finished their meal, Walter asked to be excused, and immediately went to his room.

As soon as he was gone the pastor said, "Lillian, did you notice how Walter acted to-night? It seemed to me that he was very much more thoughtful than usual."

"Yes," answered the mother, "he seemed confused, and his eyes were so bright, but he ate a very hearty supper."

"I also noticed that," said the pastor, then added, "It seems there is a change, but I hardly know whether to say the change is for better or worse. I hope it is for the best; it may be that the medicine has just taken effect."

"God grant that this may be so," reverently said the mother. They were both silent for some time, then the pastor said, "I never heard Walter speak as he did this noon. I wonder how he thought of such an absurd thing, as sending me to jail because some one else stole some chickens."

"I know, James, that it does seem absurd at first thought, yet it seems to me to be just as sensible to punish the wrong person for stealing, as it would be to punish the innocent with sickness because some one else had sinned. I have been thinking seriously of this all the afternoon, but have not arrived at a satisfactory conclusion," said Mrs. Williams.

The pastor slowly turned toward his wife and said, "Lillian I am astonished beyond measure to hear this from you; it was bad enough to hear it from my own son, but to hear it from you is worse. Don't you think that Almighty God knows what is best for us, do you dare question anything He does? Do you think the allwise Creator would have made him sick if it were not for the best?"

"James, do you really believe God made our boy sick?"

"It must be so," answered James, "for we read in the Bible, that God made everything that was made."

"If this be true James, it would be a sin to give him medicine, for we would be trying to undo the work of God."

To say the pastor was astonished would be putting it mildly. Never in his whole life had he been so shocked as on this day, and each shock was greater than the preceding one.

He now stood perfectly still for a full minute, then said, "It seems high time that we begin the study of the Bible in this house, for from what I have heard to-day it is very apparent to me that my wife and son are quite ignorant of what the Bible contains." Then turning, he strode from the room.

The pastor was a good and kind man. He had always been a good husband and father, always patient and sympathetic with his invalid wife and son; but this day had been a very trying one to him, first in hearing his son say things that he considered little less than blasphemous, then to notice that the mother seemed to indorse what the son had said, and to make matters worse, to actually hear his wife questioning the doings of God, as he understood them. This was the last-straw. He was really angry and out of patience, and somewhat confused, so he decided to go to his library and think it all over. As soon as he arrived there he impatiently seated himself in an easy chair and began to soliloquize after this fashion: "I wonder where Walter got that idea about sending me to jail, what can that have to do with his sickness; then to think my wife agreed with him. Let me see, what did she say? I was so outraged I can scarcely recall what was said. I believe though she said something about some of the apostles doubting at times. What has that to do with sending me to jail? I don't seem able to think clearly to-day. Then this other matter, about giving medicine being a sin. Why everybody takes medicine; the most pious and devout Christians that ever lived have taken medicine, and this has been so for thousands of years. The Bible says that the leaves of the trees are for the healing of the nations. Then why may not the roots and the bark be used as well? Of course Jesus Christ did not heal with medicine. He was the Son of God and was endowed from on high with supernatural power. He didn't need the medicine. Well, all I can say is that I am glad we are going to have those Bible lessons, for I

William W. Walter

know that as soon as we get to studying them they will get the truth, and then I will hear no more of this nonsense. I don't think I will mention the matter again until we get to studying the lessons; then as we get to this medicine question, I will point it out to them."

So the pastor, after having thought himself into a better frame of mind, dismissed the subject from his thoughts, arose, and walked over to the bookcase, selected the book he wanted, and was soon absorbed in reading.

In the meantime Walter had hurried to his room and was soon busily engaged in reading "Science and Health."

About nine o'clock he heard his father and mother coming upstairs to retire for the night. He hastily turned out his light and scrambled into bed, clothes and all.

A few moments later when his mother looked in she found him in bed nicely covered up, and supposing him asleep, quietly left the room. As soon as Walter was sure they had retired, he arose, relit the gas, and continued reading. It was after midnight when he laid down the book and said, "I feel sure this book is true, and that God made only the good, and never made me or any one else sick. I believe I will get well when I understand how to pray aright." Then he undressed and got into bed, a happier and more hopeful boy than he had ever been.

After saying his usual prayers, he added, "And now, God, I wish to thank you for all the good things you have given me. I could not thank you this morning, for then I thought you had made me sick. But now I know that you are all good and could not make evil; truly I now have something to be thankful for and shall always remember this Thanksgiving day."

CHAPTER IV

PREPARING FOR THE LESSONS

The next morning, when Walter awoke it was broad daylight, and the hands on the clock pointed to the hour of ten, as his mother came into his room with an anxious look on her face and said, "I have just come up to wake you as your father was worried because of your sleeping so long; how do you feel this morning?"

"Oh, mother, I feel better this morning, and I had the best night's rest I have had for years. I never woke up once all night, and I feel strong and hungry."

"Thank God you are better, I will go down and get your breakfast ready."

"All right, mother, I will be down as soon as I wash and dress." Before going down, he went over to his trunk, took out "Science and Health," and said, "I believe that you contain the truth and will free me of this disease." He then placed it in his trunk again, being careful to hide it from the view of any one who should carelessly look into it.

Hastily descending to the dining-room, he ate a hearty breakfast. As he was leaving the table his mother said, "I am sorry you did not take advantage of the beautiful sunshine yesterday, for the wind has changed and is now blowing severely from the north and it is very cold and dreary out."

"I don't mind it at all to-day, mother, for I feel so much better that I hadn't noticed the weather."

His mother was somewhat astonished to hear him speak so cheerfully, as it had been customary for Walter to complain of feeling worse on dreary days. Then she thought, "It must be that new medicine, for he certainly is better, and I pray God he will continue to improve."

As for Walter, he was glad it was a dreary day, as this would give him an excuse for staying in his room and continue his reading. He wished he was there now, but did not want to awaken the suspicion of his mother by too hurried a departure. So he walked about the room, trying to think of some excuse. Finally a happy thought occured to him, and he said, "Mother, I believe I will take the Bible and go to my room and read, so as to be prepared for our lesson this evening."

"Very well, Walter, you will find it on the library table."

Walter walked into the library, secured the book, then went up to his room, took out "Science and Health" and was soon absorbed in its contents.

The afternoon was a repetition of the morning.

At the supper table the Rev. Williams said, "I am sorry we cannot start our Bible lessons for a few evenings, as I have received a notification to be present at some meetings to be held by the local clergy."

"Any matter of importance, James?" asked his wife.

"Not particularly so. The Rev. Mr. Johnson said that they wished to find a way to successfully combat this new heretical idea called Christian Science, and they want to arrange so that each clergyman will give a sermon denouncing it, each on a different Sunday, and Rev. Johnson asked me if I was willing to deliver a sermon on it, and I told him yes."

"Why father," said Walter, "I did not know that you had ever read or looked into Christian Science."

"No son, I never did look it up or study it, and what is more I never intend to. The Bible is good enough for me."

"But, father, how can you preach a sermon on it if you do not know what it is?"

"I did not say that I did not know what it is. I have heard enough to know that it *is not* Christian and that they claim to heal in the same way that Jesus Christ did. This claim alone proves that it is false, for Jesus Christ was the Son of God, and that is why He could heal the sick, and for any man to consider himself equal to Jesus Christ is blasphemous."

"Father did not Jesus bid His disciples heal the sick?"

"Yes, certainly, He gave His disciples the power to heal the sick, but His disciples have been dead for a long time, and nobody else was given the power to heal as Christ did," said the pastor. "Was St. Paul one of Christ's disciples?"

"No Walter, he was not in reality one of Christ's disciples, but he was a very good and holy man."

"Did not St. Paul heal the sick?"

"Yes, there are several accounts in the Bible of St. Paul's healing power."

"Well father, where did St. Paul get his power to heal the sick if he was not one of the disciples that Jesus gave the power of healing to?"

"Why you see it was like this - that is - I mean to say - " the pastor stopped rather confused, then finished with, "It is too long a story to tell to-night, as I must be getting ready for that meeting. I will explain this all when we start our lessons."

The pastor left the room and entered the library, thinking deeply. "I wonder where that boy gets those queer ideas from. I am very much pleased that I suggested those Bible lessons, for if he was not enlightened, he would surely go astray."

Shortly after, the pastor was wending his way to the meeting, still thinking of what Walter had said regarding St. Paul. Walter made an excuse to retire to his room and was soon reading in his precious "Science and Health;" and it was precious to him, for in it he saw the only hope he had ever had of getting well. He read far into the night, and every spare moment of the next few days, so that when Wednesday evening came he had finished the book. But Wednesday evening was prayer meeting, so there would be no Bible lessons until Thursday evening.

He spent almost all day Thursday reading Genesis in the Bible and comparing it with the scientific interpretation as found in "Science and Health," by Mary Baker G. Eddy, under the subject of Genesis, beginning on page 501.

About six o'clock his mother called him for supper, and as he laid down his books he said, "It must be true; I feel that it is the truth. I will have father start with Genesis to-night and will ask such questions as will be most apt to get father to see the Bible in its true light. How I wish I had found this book long ago, then I would be better prepared to convince father. Still I know that God is good and will help me, and with Him to help me I cannot fail."

CHAPTER V

THE FIRST LESSON

It was just 7:30 p.m. when the pastor, his wife, and Walter entered the library to have their first Bible lesson.

"Well, Walter," said the father pleasantly, "have you decided where we shall commence our studies?"

"Yes, father, I should like to start at the beginning, with Genesis."

The pastor looked at his son and noticed that his face was flushed with excitement. Still he made no comment about it, but answered, "very well Walter, if agreeable to mother, we will start with Genesis."

"Yes, James, I am satisfied to start anywhere that pleases Walter."

"As we are all in accord, I will start with chapter 1 of Genesis, and continue reading until we come to something that you do not understand. Then you may stop me and I will explain. I think this will be an excellent way, don't you, Walter?"

"Yes, father, I think that will be the best way." The

pastor started to read Genesis, chapter 1, and there was no interruption until he arrived at Genesis 1, 26.

Several times Walter was on the point of asking some question, but did not. Now he asked, "father, what is meant by that verse? I do not understand it clearly."

"I'll read it again for you," said the pastor. "Genesis, chapter 1, 26th verse. *'And God said, let us make man in our image after our likeness, and let them have dominion over the fish of the sea and the fowl of the air and over the cattle, and over all the earth, and over every creeping thing that creepeth upon the earth.'* Do you understand it now?"

"Not yet. God is Spirit, is He not?"

"Certainly, why do you ask?"

"That verse says that God made man in His image and likeness, does that mean that man is spiritual?"

"Yes," answered the pastor. "Then my body must be spiritual."

"Oh, no, our bodies are not spiritual, it is only the soul that is in the body that is here spoken of as the image and likeness of God."

"Then God did not make our bodies, did He, father?"

"Why, certainly He did. Have you never read that God made all that was made?"

"It doesn't say anything in that verse about God's making a body does it father?"

"No but it says 'in His image and likeness,' that means just like Him," said the pastor.

"Then if I am just like Him, He in turn must be just like me, and in that case God would have a material body, and would not be wholly spirit."

"Why son, what queer ideas you have. As I said before this verse is only speaking of the soul; you will see farther on where He created the body. Now let us proceed."

"Father, what is meant by that part of this same verse, where it reads: '*And let them have dominion over the fish of the sea and the fowl of the air*,' etc.?"

"There has been considerable differences of opinion in regard to that passage. Personally, I think it means that we will have this dominion after we die and enter the spirit world, for we certainly haven't dominion over the fish and fowl here."

"James, do you think there will be fish and fowl in heaven?" meekly asked his wife.

"That is a very absurd question. Everybody knows there will be no fish and fowl in heaven," said her husband.

"Then how can we have dominion over them if there are none there?" asked his wife.

"It seems to me that you are both very dense this evening. Let us continue and these things will clear up as we proceed," said the pastor, a little nettled at his inability to answer their questions clearly.

Walter had several more questions he wanted to ask on this subject, but he thought best not to ask too many at one time.

There was no more interruption until the pastor reached Genesis 1, 31st verse - "*and God saw everything He had made, and behold it was very good, and the evening and the morning were the 6th day.*" Here Walter interrupted with, "Then everything that God made was good."

"Yes, everything that God made was good," answered the pastor.

"If that be true, God could not have made me sick, for sickness is not good," said Walter.

"Walter, I believe you are right," said his mother.

The pastor looked from one to the other, then slowly laid the Bible down in his lap. He was surprised at the turn the conversation had taken, and he remembered that Walter had on a previous occasion said something similar. Just what would be the best answer to make he did not know, so thought he would ask Walter a few questions, and in this way find out what the boy had on his mind. So he asked, "What makes you so positive that God did not make you sick Walter?"

"Because God is good and just, and I am His child, and the Bible says He made everything good and He made everything that was made, so everything must be good. Besides, I cannot conceive of a just God making me suffer for a sin some one else committed, any more than I could think of you, father, punishing me for something that our neighbor's boy had done."

Like a flash the pastor saw now what the boy had meant when he spoke of sending him to jail because some one else had stolen some chickens. The boy was only trying to illustrate to him the injustice of punishing one person for the deeds of another. Then the thought came, "Shall man be more just than God?" There was something here he did not understand, and yet the Bible said God made everything that was made. If this be true, He was the author of all the sorrows and woes, as well as the joys, of the human race.

Now that he had got to thinking on this subject, he did not like to admit even to himself that God was the creator of all the wickedness of the world. He decided he must have more time to think about this before he could answer the boy, so said, "We know that God is good and just, and some of the things that to us seem evil and unjust may still be for our good." He then picked up the Bible to proceed with his reading.

Walter noticed that his father was ill at ease and decided not to ask any more questions at present. The pastor then read Genesis 2, 1st verse: *"Thus the heavens and earth were finished and all the hosts of them."* He now cast an anxious look over at Walter, expecting him to ask some question that would be as hard to answer as the previous ones, but Walter was sitting perfectly still listening attentively.

The pastor then read the next verse, Genesis 2, 2nd verse: *"And on the seventh day God ended His work which He had made; and He rested on the seventh day from all His work which He had made"*

"Is that all of creation, father?" asked Walter.

"Yes, God created everything in six days and on the seventh He rested; that is why we observe the Sabbath day as a day of rest."

There was no interruption in the next three verses, although Walter heard several things he would like to have asked about. But when it came to Genesis 2, 6th verse, *"But there went up a mist from the earth and watered the whole face of the ground,"* Walter asked, "What is meant by that *mist*, father?" The pastor tried to find some reasonable answer, but could not, so he replied, "I suppose it was something like the fogs we sometimes see rising from the ground." He had come to the conclusion that these Bible lessons were not going to be quite so easy and entertaining as he had anticipated, and had determined that on the morrow he would go over the lesson by himself, and in this way be prepared for any and all questions that might be asked.

Walter knew what this *mist* meant; he had read all about it, in "Science and Health," but still he did not think it policy to say anything more on the subject just then. The pastor continued his reading, Genesis 2, 7th verse. *"And the Lord God formed man of the dust of the ground, and breathed into his nostrils the breath of life, and man became a living soul."*

"Will you please explain that verse to me, father?"

"With pleasure; this is the verse I spoke of a little while back, when I told you that in Genesis 1.26, God only made the soul or spirit of man, while here is a record of the creation of the body.

"You see, son, we get a better understanding as we

proceed. It is like this, the soul or spirit is in the image and likeness of God, but the body is not, it being material, having been created of dust. Do you understand it better now?"

Walter did not answer at once, so his mother said, "That all seems very plain to me now, although I was somewhat confused before."

The pastor turned a smiling face to her and nodded his head approvingly; he was now quite at his ease again, and did not look for any further trouble. Then turning to Walter, he was a little surprised to see him looking flushed and excited, so said, "Well, Walter, what are you thinking about?"

The boy looked up and said, "I was trying to think, when God started His second creation, for He had finished His first one on the sixth day and rested from His work on the seventh day, and here seems to be a record of something He created after He had finished."

Had a bomb shell exploded in the room, it would not have surprised and shocked the pastor and his wife so much as that which they had just heard; and coming just at the time when the pastor thought he was making everything clear and plain, it confused him terribly, and in his ears kept ringing what Walter had said: "I was trying to think, when God started His second creation, for He had finished His first one on the sixth day and rested from His work which He had made, on the seventh day." What could this mean; where did Walter get these queer thoughts from; were they in reality queer? The idea of a second creation was absurd, yet the Bible said, Genesis 2. 1, *"thus the heavens and earth were finished and all the hosts of them."* There it was plain enough, it spoke both of heaven and earth, *"and on the seventh day God ended His work which He had made, and He rested on the seventh day from all His work which He had made."* Did God make a mistake in the first creation and so start in again to rectify His mistake? Impossible. God was, is, and always will be all-knowing; this precluded all chance of Deity making a mistake. Was the Bible wrong in this particular instance, if so, might it not all be wrong? This thought made the good man's heart stand still. No, no, it could not be; it must be some slight error in the translation or something of that kind - yes, it must be; how was it that he had never seen it before? Then he became conscious that his wife was asking him some question.

"James," he heard her say, "are there really two creations, one spiritual and the other material?"

What should he answer? He never was so at a loss for a reply in his whole life; there was his son and his wife, both apparently depending on him for an explanation, and he absolutely incapable of making a rational one. And then he remembered that he had said it didn't make any difference to him what part of the Bible they started with, as he was very familiar with it all. At length he said: "I don't seem capable of clear thought to-night; I think we had better stop for this time, and we will begin at this same verse to-morrow night."

Walter was sorry to see his father so confused and perplexed, and tried to think of some way to help him arrive at the truth. He was afraid to say much for fear of awakening his father's suspicion, for if his father had the least idea that he had secured his information from the Christian Science text-book, "Science and Health," with key to the scriptures, he would not have allowed him to ask any more questions, nor even voice any of his thoughts, on the subject.

Walter decided to try to show his father a way out of his dilemma, so he said: "Father, don't you think your explanation about that *mist* that is spoken of in Genesis, 2. 6, being a fog is wrong?"

"What else could it be, Walter?"

"Have you ever noticed, father, that this particular verse starts in with a '*but*'? It reads, 'But there went up a mist,' it does not say, 'God made a mist to rise from the earth.'"

"I don't see that the word 'but' changes it any."

"I did not mean to say that it did, I only wished to point out the fact that here was something that God did not make, for nowhere in the preceding chapters of Genesis had God made a mist."

"I cannot understand what you mean, Walter. The Bible says that God made everything that was made, and as I have seen a mist many times, God must have made it as there is only one Creator," said the pastor.

"On the same line of reasoning, we would have to admit God created all the evils of this world, for we see these evils every day, and then I would have to admit that God made me sick, and I can never believe that, for Genesis 1, 31st verse reads, '*And God saw everything that He had made, and behold it was very good*.' If we believe this, we cannot possibly believe

He made any evil thing."

"Well Walter, we will not discuss that subject farther at the present time, for I know as we progress with our lessons you will see it in a different light; anyway I don't see what that mist has to do with the subject."

"Father, might not that mist mean a mistake or a misapprehension? Then that verse would read, 'But there went up a misapprehension from the earth, and watered the whole face of the ground.'"

"Why, Walter there would be no sense to such a speech; how could a misapprehension water the whole face of the ground?" "Is not the Bible supposed to be an inspired book, father?"

"Yes, certainly."

"And is there not supposed to be a spiritual meaning to all there is written there?"

"Yes, Walter, why do you ask?"

"Then might not the spiritual meaning of that verse be brought out by using the word 'arose' instead of 'went up,' and the word 'deceived,' instead of 'watered,' and the word 'intelligence,' in place of 'face,' and the word 'people,' instead of 'ground'; then the verse would read like this, 'But there arose a misapprehension from the earth and deceived the whole intelligence of the people.' If we add to this what is implied, that the following creation is what the people through this misapprehension believe, we get a clearer view of the real creation as narrated in the first chapter of Genesis."

It was several moments after Walter finished speaking before the pastor or his wife made any reply. Many times that evening they had been surprised at what they had heard Walter say, now they were both surprised and bewildered. The mother was the first to speak and said: "What you say, Walter, seems reasonable, yet I do not think we have the right to change anything that is written in the Bible."

"That is true, wife, it is from this pernicious habit of translating the Bible to suit the thought of each ignoramus that thinks he knows something of the Bible, simply because he has read it once or twice, that all the contradictory sayings about the Bible originate, and it ought to be stopped by law," said the pastor.

"Why, father, that is not changing the Bible, it is simply bringing to light the hidden meaning, the same as you do when you interpret some of the sayings, or parables, of Jesus; anyway, I merely suggested that this might be the solution of the question of a second creation."

"Walter do not speak of a second creation again; everybody knows there is only one creation for there is only one God and He is omniscient; that precludes the thought of a mistake and a re-creation. God made everything that was made in six days, and if He made everything in that time, there would not be anything more to make; for 'everything' includes, 'all.'" "Then which of the two narratives in the Bible is the true one, James?" asked his wife.

"My dear, this second narrative is the same creation, told in a more simple way so that all may understand.

It enters into the details and tells *how* God created everything."

The pastor had not intended giving such an explanation as this when he started to speak, but this thought occurred to him and it seemed reasonable, so he voiced it, and now that he said it, he felt satisfied that the first creation was the real creation, and that the second narrative was the explanation of how everything was created.

Walter was somewhat confused by his father's explanation. He had never thought of it in this light, and now he was at a loss what to say. He felt sure that his father's explanation was not the correct solution, yet he could not find words to express his thoughts. Then he thought of his precious "Science and Health"; if I could only look into that for a few minutes, I know I could find the true explanation; then turning to his father he said: "Don't you think we have had enough Bible study for the first night? It is half past nine.

"Why, how fast the evening has passed. I'm sure you must be tired," anxiously exclaimed his mother.

"Yes, Walter," said his father, "it is time that we retire, for there are many more evenings this winter, and we must not think we can learn all the Bible contains in one evening. I hope I made that second narrative plain to you."

"I am not fully convinced that we have arrived at the truth of this second creation, father. I shall spend to-morrow thinking and studying on that subject, and maybe by to-morrow evening I will be able to see it as it really is."

"That's right, Walter," said the pastor, highly pleased at the thought of his son taking such an interest in the scriptures, "it is only by study and research that we can gain knowledge." The pastor had no idea that Walter had any other source of information than the family Bible, but Walter was thinking of his key to the scriptures by Mrs. Eddy, with which he proposed to unlock the treasure vaults of the Bible. "Come, Walter, you had better go to bed, I fear you have already overexerted yourself, as you are not accustomed to being up so late."

Walter turned a bright and cheery face to her and said, "I do not feel tired at all mother, for the lesson has been very interesting to me, so do not worry. I am sure it did me good." Then turning to his father, he said, "Good-night, father, shall we have another lesson to-morrow night?"

"Yes, certainly; now good-night and pleasant dreams."

Walter bade his mother an affectionate good-night and went to his room. As soon as he was gone, father and mother looked at each other and there was hope and delight written on both their faces.

"He is surely getting better," said the mother.

"I never saw him so interested and cheerful in his whole life," remarked the father.

"I think we have secured the right medicine at last," said the mother.

"I have prayed long and faithfully to God that He spare his life and guide his footsteps into the ministry, and I believe both prayers have been heard, for he is surely gaining rapidly in health, and has taken more than an ordinary interest in the Bible; some of his questions were very absurd, but this is simply because he does not understand. I shall put a little study on to-morrow's lesson, so as to be more able to explain any and all questions he may ask," said the father.

Shortly after, they ascended the stairs to retire for the night. As they passed Walter's room the mother softly opened the door, looked at her sleeping boy, silently closed the door, and said, "Dear boy, he must have been tired to fall asleep so quickly."

But Walter was not sleeping, he felt he could not sleep until he had cleared up the matter of a second creation. He also knew his mother would look into the room before she retired, so he pretended to be asleep. As soon as she had closed the door he arose and turned on the light, went to his trunk, and brought forth his "Science and Health." He then seated himself and said, "I'm sure I saw this all explained in the book; I wonder what part I will find it in; I should think it would be in the explanation of Genesis." Turning to Genesis, he read until he came to page 524, line 14, then exclaimed, "Here it is, plain as day; it wasn't God, Spirit, that created the *dust* man, and all the rest of this material universe. It was the Lord God, that is, man's material conception of God, or false God. I wonder how I am going to make this plain to father without showing him my 'Science and Health.'" Then putting away his book he was soon in bed and asleep.

CHAPTER VI

CONFUSION

The next morning as soon as breakfast was over, the pastor went to the library, secured his Bible, and began to read. After reading for some time, a look of perplexity came over his face; he leaned back in his chair, thinking deeply, and his thoughts were as follows: It's remarkable that I never noticed this second narrative is the reverse of the first; they are clearly and distinctly two narratives. In the first there is no mention made of anything material, and all is created by the word of God - or spiritually; there is no mention of evil, but - all is pronounced good by God. He made the earth, the trees, and the animals first, and man last, in an ascending scale; while in the 2d chapter of Genesis, God is supposed to have made man first, then woman, then the animals, etc., in a descending scale. I am now quite sure my explanation to Walter about this second creation being a more detailed account of the first is not correct, yet what else could it be? It certainly cannot be a second creation. Let me see, what did Walter say about that *mist* being a misapprehension that arose among the people as to creation? And that this second narrative was the misapprehension? It sounded reasonable and would be an easy solution to this second creation; but how about this material body of mine, and the rest of the material things? Are we

William W. Walter

laboring under a misapprehension regarding all these things? Impossible, we could not all make the same mistake; yet according to Walter's explanation this *mist* watered the whole face of the earth; that means all the people. Where did this mist or misapprehension come from? There is no record of God having made it. What a position for a minister of the gospel to be in, unable to explain the simplest things regarding creation; preaching that man is the image and likeness of God, who is Spirit, and believing man was created out of *dust* or materially, thereby contradicting the statement, that we are the image and likeness of God, Spirit; for matter is not spirit, but its opposite. I must admit I am very much confused, and I must be able to explain by to-night, for Walter will be disappointed if he cannot continue his lesson this evening. I think I had better read these first two chapters of Genesis over a few more times, and maybe I will be able to see through this confusion.

The pastor read and studied until dinner was called, then the entire afternoon. When he laid his book down to come to supper he said, "I am fully convinced that these two narratives are not meant to be the same, nor is one the explanation of the other, for one is the direct opposite of the other. But I cannot decide which is the real, for the Bible speaks as though God was the author of both. Maybe Walter will have some idea that will shed light on the subject. I am astonished at his explanation of that mist; it is so reasonable. It is remarkable that it never occured to me, after the many times I have read it."

At the supper table the pastor said, "Walter, what have you been doing all day? I haven't seen you except at dinner, and now at supper."

"I have been reading and thinking preparatory to our lesson, as I suppose we will have another lesson this evening."

"Yes, Walter, we will continue, although I must confess I am not as well prepared as I should like to be."

"Why, James, I thought you were reading the Bible almost all day," said his wife.

"So I was, dear, but could not fully satisfy myself as to that second narrative being an explanation of the first; in fact, I came to the conclusion that it was not, but that it is a separate, and distinct narrative."

"Do you mean to say that there really were two creations?" asked his wife in a surprised tone.

"No, dear, I do not mean that; the fact of the matter is, I cannot find any reasonable solution for there being two accounts of creation, and as this thought had never occured to me before, I have not been able to find a satisfactory explanation. Nevertheless, we will take this subject up in our lesson this evening, and see if we cannot explain it satisfactorily to all concerned. I am going to the library, and when you are ready you can both come there, and we will get an early start." The pastor then quitted the room.

Mrs. Williams turned to her son and said, "Walter, I cannot understand how your father can be confused at anything he could find in the Bible, for he was credited with being one of the best Bible students in this part of the country."

"I suppose, mother, that it had never occurred to father, that there were two accounts of creation in the Bible, and possibly it had never been pointed out to him. I think though, that before the evening lesson is over we will all understand just why that second account is given. Personally, I have come to a satisfactory conclusion concerning it, and maybe father will agree with me."

"Now, Walter, you must not presume to teach your father anything concerning the Bible; he has put years of hard study on it."

"I know that is true, mother, but it has often happened that a skilled mechanic has worked for years on some particular thing, and never attained what he was after, and some other person who knew nothing of mechanism discovered the solution without any trouble. It may be so in this case, you or I may say just the thing that will clear up this seeming mystery."

"I know that such things have happened, but I would hardly presume to be able to say anything in regard to the Bible that your father has not thought of years ago."

Walter did not wish to say anything more on this subject at present, but it had occured to him that if his father had been taught wrong in regard to creation, most likely he had also been mis-taught in regard to the rest of the Bible, for he reasoned that if he started to explain the Bible from the wrong standpoint, that is materially, instead of spiritually, he would necessarily be in error as to the truth of all the teachings of the Bible.

CHAPTER VII

THE SECOND LESSON

It was not long before his mother had finished her work. She then said, "Come, Walter, I am ready now to go to the library."

They both entered and found Mr. Williams waiting for them with the Bible open in his hand. He looked up at them as soon as they appeared and said, "I suppose the great question before the class to-night is to decide whether there are one or two creations chronicled in the Bible; and if there are two, which one is the real. Have you arrived at any conclusion in regard to this point, Walter?"

"Yes, father, I have. It seems very plain to me now, and if you will allow me, I shall be pleased to give my views regarding these two creations."

This was just what the pastor wanted. He wished Walter to speak first, to see what conclusions the boy had arrived at, before he expressed his own opinion, so he readily gave his consent and said, "Speak your mind freely, son, and if I cannot agree with you on all points, we will take up those points afterwards and discuss them."

William W. Walter

Walter now had the privilege he wanted, but he felt he must be careful not to say too much for fear of awakening his father's suspicion; so he quietly opened the Bible he had brought with him, and read aloud, Genesis 2, 7th verse, "*And the Lord God formed man of the dust of the ground and breathed into his nostrils the breath of life, and man became a living soul.*" As he finished reading this verse, he looked at his father and said, "You will notice, father, that the Bible says, 'the *Lord God*' formed this dust man, and this is not the same God that created man in his image and likeness. You will also notice that in the first narrative it simply speaks of God creating everything, and in the second narrative it always speaks of the *Lord God* as having made everything and - "

"Wait, Walter," said the pastor hurriedly. He had intended to let Walter say everything he had to say on the subject, but he could not think of allowing his son to bring out the theory that there were two Gods, as this would be worse than the thought of two creations. "You surely are not trying to bring forth the theory that there are two Gods, two supreme powers. I cannot possibly allow you to advance such a thought even in theory, for that would be pantheism."

"Please, father, let me finish my explanation. I have no intention of bringing forth a theory upholding two supreme powers, but I desire to show that we are now believing in two supreme powers, and that only one is true and real. Will you please look at the verse I have just read? Notice that it uses the words, *Lord God*, and you will find that this form is used almost all of the way through this second narrative. Now look at the first chapter of Genesis; you will notice that it never speaks of the *Lord God*, but simply of God."

The pastor had caught the meaning of what Walter had said, and was now diligently reading first a verse in chapter 1, Genesis, then a corresponding verse in chapter 2.

Walter's mother had quietly risen, gone to the bookcase, secured a Bible and was also comparing one with the other. At length the pastor looked up at Walter with a surprised and confused look, and said, "What you say is true, Walter, and I must admit I never noticed this before, but I cannot see that it changes the narratives any. The author or writer simply changed the name he employed to designate Deity, that is all. Still I cannot understand what his reason could have been for making the change. It is also remarkable that the change should take place just at the time it does, at the beginning of the second narrative."

"It does seem strange that such a change should be made, if it was not done for a purpose," said Mrs. Williams.

"I believe I can explain why the change was made," said Walter.

"Very well, Walter," said the pastor, "let us hear your explanation."

"Well, father, as I understand it, the first creation is real, it being the work of God. Then the Bible speaks of that *mist* or misapprehension that arose, and the story told in the second narrative is this misapprehension. Therefore, I should judge that *Lord God* would mean a man-conceived God; and man, through misapprehending the real character and nature of Deity, believes the earth and man were created according to the second narrative, which would agree with all our present ideas. I mean by this that we all think and believe that God made man materially out of the dust of the earth, while the first account says man was made in the image and likeness of God; and as God is Spirit, man must be spiritual; as a dust or material man cannot be that likeness, because matter is the opposite of spirit. Then again, everything that God made was good - and this dust man is more evil than good; and as God, who is conceded as being all good, made all, and pronounced all He made good, this dust or material man, being evil, was never made, but, through a misapprehension, we think man to be material, and believe him to be the real man. To illustrate what I mean, say some one told you a falsehood and you believed it to be the truth; then the lie would seem true to you. Nevertheless, because you believe this lie to be the truth, it would not make a truth of it, as it would be a lie still, regardless of your belief. In the same way theologists have made a mistake by thinking that this second creation is the real, and have taught all mankind that they originated from dust and must return to dust, and every one believes this; and because every one believes this mistake, it seems like the truth to all of us, but no matter how many believe a lie, it does not make a truth of it; and it is because of this false interpretation that all evil has come upon us, for in the real and spiritual creation there is no mention of evil. It is only after that mist or misapprehension arose that evil is mentioned. Oh, father, if my explanation is the truth, then God did not make evil, did not make sickness; and if He didn't make sickness, it was never made, for the Bible says, God made all that was made, then sickness is also a part of the misapprehension that arose, and is not real, does not exist, only in our mistaken thoughts. In other words, we have all been taking a lie for the truth, and the whole world has been taught this error, and through this mistake we thought it possible for evil to exist when we ought to have known that God could not have made evil, for there is no mention of sin, disease, or death in the first narrative, or real creation."

Walter stopped, his face all aglow with joy and happiness. He had risen to his feet while he was speaking and now he looked from father to mother, but he only saw perplexity written on their faces.

"Can't you see it, father? mother, didn't I make it plain? It seems so easy for me to understand it now; don't you see what it means to me? It means that I never was sick in reality, that I never need be sick in reality, that I am sick only in belief, that all any one need do to get well is to find out this truth, that sickness is only an illusion, a lie, which the truth will correct. This must be the truth that Jesus Christ spoke of when He said, Ye shall know the truth, and the truth shall make you free. Yes, it has made me free, for it has lifted this cloud of sickness and feebleness from my mind, and I feel perfectly well and strong."

Again he looked from one to the other of his parents, on his father's face he saw sorrow written, on his mother's fear.

Walter then turned his face upward, and said, "Oh, thou, God, who is all good, who never made evil or sickness, I thank thee for this great truth which thou hast revealed to me. I also desire that thou show this same truth to my father and mother, and I believe that thou wilt, for thy Son, Jesus Christ, hath said that whatever we desire when we pray, we should believe that we receive and we would receive; and I do believe that my desire will be granted, for Jesus Christ would not have said it if it were not true."

The Rev. Mr. Williams and his good wife were speechless. The words they had heard and the actions of Walter had caused the father to fear that his son's mind had given way; while the mother thought there was something supernatural about it all, and she felt half inclined to believe that what she had heard was the truth, and that this wisdom was given to her son from on high.

Now the pastor advanced to where Walter stood, looked at him inquiringly, laid his hand on his arm, and said, "Sit down, Walter, don't get excited about this question; we will all understand it better after a while." Then looking at his wife, he said, "Mother, don't you think we have had enough Bible lesson for this evening?"

His wife was surprised at the question, for she had not thought of Walter as being demented. She could not see why the pastor wished to discontinue the lesson, for they had only begun; but, ever ready to agree with her husband, she answered, "Just as you think, James."

Walter looked at his father for a moment, wondering what could be the matter, and as he thought of all he had said, it occured to him that his father must think he had lost his reason; this struck him as so ridiculous that he burst out laughing, more heartily than he had ever done in his life, for he felt better and more free than ever before. But his laughter only made matters worse as it confirmed his father's opinion in regard to his having lost his reason; and now the good man sadly shook his head, saying, "It is worse than I thought."

This only made Walter laugh the heartier.

The mother looked from her laughing son to her sorrowing husband, wondering what it all meant. At last she said, "James, what is worse than you thought?"

Before the pastor could answer, Walter said, "Mother, father thinks I have gone crazy, and this seemed so ridiculous to me that I could not control my laughter."

"Crazy!" ejaculated the mother, "did you think that, James?"

The pastor did not answer. He had supposed that no one but a demented person would say the things Walter had said, but it certainly was not the act of a demented person to guess what he had thought.

"Mother," said Walter, and there was still a healthy smile on his face, "now that I come to think of it, I do not wonder that father thought I had lost my reason, as it would be impossible for him to grasp this great truth as readily as you or I. To do so, he would have to unlearn in these few minutes all that he had ever learned regarding this false creation; with you and I, mother, it would be easier; we only believed, and belief is never absolute conviction, and can more readily be changed. I read a parable to-day that I think will explain what I mean. Jesus said, '*you cannot add any more to a cask already full.*' So it is with father; his mind is filled so full of the present idea of God and this material creation, that there cannot enter anything different from this teaching, until some of the old is emptied out. I believe this emptying out process is

William W. Walter

what is meant by Jesus when He said, *'unless ye become as little children, you can in no wise enter the kingdom of heaven.'* I take this to mean that we must put human opinion and prejudice aside, and have a free, open, and inquiring mind before this great truth can be understood by us."

"Walter," said his father rather sternly, "I think you have said enough on this question. Do you think it common sense for you to put yourself up as a greater authority as to what the Bible means than all the great men who have labored all their lives on the Bible? I do not wonder that I thought for a moment you had lost your reason, as I do not think any sane person would advance such a chimerical idea, and claim it to be the truth, as you have done. I see I have made a mistake in allowing you to question the Bible. Hereafter, I shall read from the Bible and explain it as we proceed, but I will not allow any more comments to be made. In regard to this question of creation, we will consider that closed for the present, and in the near future, probably next Sunday, I will preach a sermon on creation; and as you will undoubtedly both be there, you will see this question made plain. In the meantime I think we will discontinue the lesson, so as to give you a chance to study the Bible. I was not aware that you knew so little of what it contained, for you do not seem to grasp the simplest statements when I explain them to you."

Walter was very much astonished at the way his father had taken his explanation, and for a moment was sorry that he had said so much at one time; then he smiled as a happy thought struck him. If his father intended to deliver a thorough sermon on creation, he would be compelled to carefully study Genesis, and Walter believed enough had been said to make his father doubt the second narrative. He felt like saying, "I don't believe you will ever preach that sermon," but instead, he said, "Alright, father, I shall put considerable study on the Bible, as you wish and I am sorry if my explanation has offended you, yet I explained it just as it seemed to me."

"Never mind, Walter," said his mother, "we cannot all of us be as well versed on the Bible as your father, who has spent most of his life in the study of it."

"Would you suggest, father, that I continue to study Genesis from the place we left off?"

"Yes son," said the pastor more kindly, "start from where we left off this evening, and it might be well for you to review what we have passed over, so you will be able to fully understand my sermon when I deliver it."

After a few more commonplace remarks, Walter bade his father and mother good night, and ascended to his chamber, carrying his Bible with him.

As soon as Walter had left the room, the pastor turned to his wife and said, "I wonder what can have taken possession of that boy, he has changed wonderfully. Whereas he was always speaking of his sickness, and complaining of being weak, he now never refers to his trouble, nor does he complain of being tired any more. And what is more wonderful, he does not walk and act as if he was tired or weak; he also looks cheerful and his explanation was full of vim and courage, even though it was nonsense."

"I think, James, it is the work of that last medicine. He has begun to notice that he is getting better, and in his great enthusiasm he ascribes his healing to the goodness of God, and is very desirous of giving thanks for his recovery."

"That may be it," said the pastor, "yet I don't see any reason for his talking such nonsense. Some of his assertions are simply absurd; for instance, that assertion about his never having been sick in reality, and that there is no evil; haven't we had the best physicians in the country, and didn't they say he had hereditary consumption. That certainly ought to prove its reality. Besides, he has been gradually growing weaker and weaker under our very eyes."

"That is all true, James, yet I do not think all he said was nonsense. It seemed to me that when he was speaking he seemed to glow with a heavenly radiance, and while you thought he had lost his mind, I supposed he was inspired from on high."

The pastor sat bolt upright in his chair, and looked at his wife. If this thing kept up much longer he would be demented himself; what was the matter with his family? How could his wife take the nonsense of a boy for inspiration?

"Now, James, don't look at me that way; it does not seem so very incredible to me that God should have made everything good, and that the good alone is real, and that evil is unreal, but that we make a reality of it simply by thinking it real. I think that is what Walter was trying to make clear to us. To illustrate, if you should receive word this evening that your brother was killed in a railroad disaster, you would certainly feel sorrowful, and you would say you felt that way because your brother was killed. Now if in the morning your brother should step in the house perfectly well, your sorrow would flee. This would prove that your sorrow was not caused by the death of your brother, but simply because you believed him dead; so it was the belief that caused the sorrow, and not the deed itself." "I can agree with you in regard to your illustration, for it was the belief of my brother's death, and not his real death, as he did not die, that made me sorrowful. But the two cases are not parallel; in the one, nothing had happened, but in the other there is in reality a sick boy, and not simply the report of a sick boy."

"Can you not see, James, that if God never made sickness, and He made all there was made, that sickness could not be a reality? And we could not be sick in reality. Yet if we thought ourselves sick and believed what we thought, this would make it seem true to us, though in fact, it was not true. I believe it is just as Walter put it. If we believe a falsehood to be the truth, this falsehood, then, seems like the truth to us. But no matter how often, or how many, believe a lie to be the truth, it still in fact remains a lie."

"What you say about the lie, wife, is plain, but sickness is not a lie or a falsehood, it is only too real."

"James, if sin, sickness, and death are real, God must have made them, for the Bible says God made everything that was made and pronounced it all very good. It might be possible to stretch the imagination so as to say that sickness, or even death, might be good under certain conditions; but no Christian would agree with you that sin was good. And if we would agree that

William W. Walter

sickness and death were made by God and were good, then Jesus Christ destroyed the works of God, and at the same time destroyed something that was good."

"Oh, James, the more I think of Walter's explanation, the more reasonable it seems, and I cannot get the idea out of my mind that our boy was inspired when he made that explanation."

"Lillian, I will admit that never in my whole life have I been so confused on anything as I am in regard to these two narratives of creation. If we admit that the first is the real and was all that was made, whence came all this evil, sin, and sickness into the world, and how did I acquire this material body, and where did all these other material things come from? If we admit that the second creation is of God, then God, in a sense, would be responsible for all the trials and tribulations of man, for God is all-powerful and could have made us better, even to perfection. Now that I think of it, I don't believe the Bible mentions anywhere that God made evil. It speaks of the Lord God cursing the ground, but it does not accuse Him of making evil; and yet God should have made all. Can evil only be a lie, a dream, a delusion, a mistake or misapprehension, as Walter called it? What a state for a minister to be in; why, I believe I am questioning the truth of the Bible."

"No, James, I don't think you could properly call that questioning the Bible, you are simply seeking the truth, and I know that when you get into a calmer frame of mind you will readily find it; don't you think we had better retire for to-night? To-morrow you will have time to look up this entire matter."

"I suppose we had, as I see no way to satisfy myself

except by carefully studying the whole book of Genesis, and I am very doubtful whether I will be able to find what I want even there, for I have often noticed that when a man once begins to doubt the truth of the Bible, he usually ends up as an unbeliever. God grant that this may not happen to me."

"O, I have no fear of that," said his wife; "you are too firm a believer in God to ever doubt anything in the Bible."

"I hope so, wife, yet I must admit that I am beginning to doubt the genuineness of the second narrative, and for the last fifteen years I have preached the gospel from the standpoint of this second or dust creation. In fact, I could not preach otherwise, as it would be impossible for me to make my congregation believe that they were wholly spiritual, and that they have no material body, had I desired."

"Why, James, of course we have a material body, don't we have to feed, clothe, and take care of it?"

"That is the way I always believed, but if Walter's idea is correct in regard to that mist, or misapprehension, then the first chapter of Genesis is correct, and in that case we could not possibly have a material body, but only think we have, and because we believe what we think, it would seem so to us. Wife, I am half inclined to think this is the solution, but how can I prove to others, or even myself, that my body is spiritual when it is so very material?"

"It is quite surprising to me, James, that you cannot readily explain this part of the Bible, for you have done little else all your life but study the Bible. At any rate, let it rest for to-night; you will, no doubt, get the right thought more readily after a good night's sleep."

The pastor rather reluctantly followed his wife out of the room and up stairs. He would have preferred to solve this knotty problem before retiring. He lay awake a long time thinking deeply, and the more he thought the more firmly he believed that Walter was right in his conclusions that the first narrative was the true one. Then the thought came; if this is correct, it will turn the whole world into confusion, for everybody believes in the dust man; in fact, every clergyman I know of is preaching the gospel from this standpoint.

It was after midnight before he finally went to sleep.

Walter, also, lay awake some time, but he was not trying to solve the question of which was the true narrative; he had fully satisfied himself in regard to this. What he was trying to do was to think of some way to convince his father and mother in regard to it.

CHAPTER VIII

THE THIRD LESSON

Nearly two months had passed since the evening of the last Bible lesson. Walter was so interested in studying the Bible and "Science and Health," that he did not notice the dreary winter days. Besides, he was gaining very rapidly in strength and flesh to the great joy of his parents. His mother had some time ago noticed that he did not take his medicine, and spoke to him about it. He answered her in a very positive, but gentle tone, "No, mother, I am not taking any medicine and never intend to take any more, for I am now depending entirely on God, and He is making me well."

His mother had asked him when he had stopped taking it, and he said, "I determined never again to take medicine the night I realized the unreality of sickness, as it would be very foolish to take medicine to cure me of something which in reality did not exist." Both his father and mother tried to persuade him to continue taking his medicine, as they believed his improvement was due to this last kind he had been taking.

Walter knew better, so had said, "Please allow me to leave off taking it for a short time, and if I do not continue to improve, I will start taking it again to please you."

William W. Walter

It had been left that way, although his parents were averse to his stopping at the very time he seemed to be gaining. They watched him closely, but he continued to improve so steadily and rapidly, that taking medicine had not been mentioned to him again. His mother continued taking hers, but showed no improvement.

Many times Walter asked his father when he would take up their Bible lessons again; but his father never seemed ready. He noticed that his father always seemed to be in a very thoughtful mood. The boy knew what was the cause of it, and several times had tried to engage his father in conversation regarding creation or some other part of the Bible, as he desired to point out the truth to him. But his father always dropped the subject as soon as possible, nor had he preached his sermon on creation as he had promised.

The pastor daily studied his Bible and was taking copious notes as he read, but did not seem to arrive at a satisfactory conclusion. Many times he wondered at the little things Walter would say about the Bible, and on several occasions he had made up his mind to ask him some questions, but he disliked to let the boy know of his own inability to understand the Bible. He wondered if his wife was right in regard to the boy's being inspired. How else could he account for some of the things Walter said. On several occasions he had taken the trouble to prove his assertions, and found to his surprise that the Bible easily substantiated what the boy had said.

This was the state of affairs on a January afternoon when the pastor said to himself, "come what will, I am going to continue those Bible lessons this evening.

What Walter said brought me into this darkness and confusion and it is possible he may say something that will show me the light."

That evening at supper the pastor surprised his wife and son by saying, "If it is agreeable to you both, we will continue our Bible lessons this evening."

They readily assented, and as soon as Mrs. Williams had finished her work, they repaired to the library.

As soon as they were seated the pastor said, "Well, Walter, have you changed your mind in regard to which of the two narratives regarding creation is the correct one?"

"No, father, I have not. I have put considerable more study on that subject since our last lesson, and I am now fully satisfied and convinced that the view expressed in regard to the first narrative being the true one is correct."

"Walter, I believe you are right. I have been studying and thinking all of these two months, and have come to the same conclusion regarding creation. Yet in no way have I been able to explain away all these material things and this material body."

"James, have you come to the conclusion that everything is spiritual?" asked his wife.

"Yes, Lillian, for there are only two conclusions to arrive at, either God is the creator spoken of in the first narrative where everything was made by the Word, or spiritually, and is pronounced very good, or else God is the creator spoken of in the second narrative and therefore He would be the creator of all this evil, sickness, sin, and death, with all the other dire calamities we are subjected to. And since I have thought and studied on this question, I cannot conceive of our Heavenly Father being the cause of all our troubles, who are His children, any more than I would bring such a visitation on my family. So of the two, I prefer believing that God made everything good as described in the first narrative, as it is impossible to believe both, for they are direct opposites. What bothers me is this material body and everything else that is material."

"Father, I believe I can throw some light on that subject if you will allow me."

His father looked at him for a moment, undecided whether to ask him to explain or not, for his last explanation had caused all his confusion, yet, as he thought of it, he now agreed with that explanation. Maybe the boy was inspired and he was doing wrong in not hearing what he had to say. Anyway, his getting well without the use of doctors or drugs was little short of a miracle to him, so he decided to have him explain, and said, "I will hear what you have to say on this subject, Walter, but be careful not to say anything ridiculous."

Walter smiled; he had learned a lesson the time he made his explanation regarding creation, and he did not intend that his enthusiasm should cause him to say too much this time and thereby make the same mistake he had made before. So he simply asked his father a question. "Did not everybody think the earth was flat years ago?"

"Yes, Walter, but what has that to do with our material bodies?"

"Did everybody believe it, father?"

"Certainly, for they did not know different"

"Did their thinking so make it so?"

"Most assuredly not, as you well know, Walter, the earth was always round."

"And even though they believed this mistake regarding the earth, it did not change the earth any, did it, father?" "No, but why these questions?"

"Only this, father, that this is just what we have been long doing regarding our bodies, thinking that they were material and believing it, but our mistaken thought regarding our bodies has not in reality changed them, any more than the thought that the earth was flat changed the earth. It seemed flat to those who believed it flat, though the truth was that the earth was round in reality. So with our bodies; they are material to us who believe them so, but in truth or reality, they are spiritual."

"I can readily agree with you in regard to the earth, because we know that it always was round, but we cannot prove that the body is spiritual."

"That is just the point, father. We can readily admit that the earth is round after it has been proven so; still before this proof was furnished the people would not admit it, any more than we will admit that our bodies are spiritual. Nevertheless the earth was round before it was proven so, and so with the body being spiritual. The proof of its spirituality does not change it any, as it will always remain as God made it, regardless of what man thinks or believes about it, nevertheless, Jesus Christ on several occasions proved the body to be spiritual and the proof that He done so is contained in the Bible, He also said 'Blessed are they who believe and do not see.'"

"I know Jesus Christ said that, but that was about something entirely different. You could hardly want me to believe something I could not see or prove, for you know, Walter, the old saying is that seeing is believing."

Walter immediately thought of what "Science and Health" said on this subject, so he said, "Can we always believe what we see?"

"Yes, I think so, son."

"Father, if you were to look out of this window to-morrow morning you would see in the distance where the heaven and earth seemed to meet; would you believe they did?"

"Certainly not, for I know better."

"Still you say, seeing is believing." His father leaned back in his chair and regarded his son critically; was the boy inspired? How else could he account for his intelligence? What was he to hear next, should he ask any more questions? Yes, he would ask him something more about this material body: "Walter is there anything in the Bible that you know of wherewith to substantiate your claim of a spiritual body?"

"I think there is, father. Jesus Christ must have known that his body was spiritual, and not material, for if his body had been material he could not have walked on the water, and in several places it speaks of Jesus becoming invisible to those around him."

"I know, son, but Jesus Christ was the Son of God."

"That is true, father, so are we, I distinctly remember reading in St. John - 'now are we the sons of God.' St. Paul also speaks of us as sons of God and joint heirs with Christ."

The Rev. Williams slowly closed the Bible he had been holding open on his knee and looked at his son. Where would this thing end? He must try and confine the boy to one thing at a time, so he said, "I am still in the dark concerning your idea of how the material body came to be."

"Father, I will quote you again from the Bible - 'as a man thinketh in his heart, so is he' This means that if you think anything, no matter what, and believe what you think, then so it is with you, and it seems true to you. For instance, take a person that is demented, who imagines he is King George, and believes it; to himself he is king George and no one can make him believe otherwise."

"That may be true of one who is demented, but how about a sane person?"

"This person may be sane on every topic but that one. Still I will give you another illustration of what the wrong thought on any subject will do. I read a while ago about some college students who decided to play a

William W. Walter

joke on their professor. This professor had several blocks to walk to the college, and the students decided to place themselves at frequent intervals along his path, and each one was to comment on how badly he looked, and intimate to him that he was sick. So on a certain morning as the professor was walking to the college (and he was feeling as well as usual), the first person he met was one of the students who greeted him warmly with a hearty 'good morning' and then added, 'What is the matter, professor, are you sick?' The professor said, 'No, I am feeling as well as usual; why do you ask?' The student then told him he looked very pale, and that he thought he must surely be sick. The professor then assured the student that he was feeling well and started toward the college. The next student he met also told him he looked sick; this was repeated several times, and caused the professor to imagine there must be something wrong. After meeting several more of the jokers he began to think he must be sick. Then being told the same thing a few more times, he believed he was sick, or believed what he thought, and turned back home a very sick man. So it is with us, we think we have material bodies, and because we believe what we think, it makes it seem true to us, even though it is not the truth."

"A very good illustration, Walter, I think I understand what you mean. If we all thought our bodies were spiritual and believed what we thought, then our bodies would be spiritual; in other words, whichever way we thought and believed, so it would really be."

"No father, that is not quite right. Simply thinking you are sick or well and believing it does not make you sick, or well, in reality; it only seems to do it to our mistaken mortal sense of things; the truth of anything remains the truth, regardless of how many falsehoods are told about it."

"Am I to understand Walter, that no matter what I or others may think or believe about this body, it does not change the facts regarding it, but only seems to do so to our senses?"

"That is just what I mean. God made us in His image and likeness, and as He is Spirit we must be like Him or spiritual, for matter is not the likeness of Spirit, but its opposite."

"That seems quite reasonable, Walter," said his mother, "but this material body is here, I can see it and feel it."

"It only seems to be material, mother, because we take our information from our five material senses; and as these five senses can only testify regarding material things because of their materiality, they do not testify to the truth, or reality, of man and the universe."

"But Walter," said the pastor, "if I am not to believe the testimony of my five senses, how am I to know anything?"

"The five material senses are continually deceiving us. The sense of sight I have spoken of before, but will give you a different illustration that shows up the deception of all the senses." "Father, do you believe life to be a reality?"

"I certainly do."

"Can you see life?"

"I hardly know how to answer that, I can see that you are alive. No, I shall say we can not see life itself, but only the manifestation of life."

"I agree with you, father, we cannot see life itself. Can we hear life?"

"No."

"Can we touch life?"

"No."

"Can we smell life?"

"No."

"Can we taste life?"

"No."

"Then our five material senses do not testify anything regarding a reality, for you said life was a reality." The pastor and his wife were very much surprised at Walter's ability to explain these things, and his mother was fully convinced of his being inspired, and the father was fast coming to the same conclusion.

"Did you understand me, father?"

"Yes, fully, you made it very plain."

"Now, father, would you say that the opposite of a reality was an unreality?"

The pastor hesitated, hardly daring to answer; at length

he said, "Yes, it must be."

"Is not death the opposite of life, father?"

"Yes, Walter."

"Then if life is real, its opposite, or death, must be unreal; can you agree with me, father?" He always addressed his father, for his mother was showing by the nod of her head that she fully agreed with him."

"I must say, Walter, that I do agree with you, to quite an extent; but, I shall have to think it all over carefully before I will be fully convinced."

Walter then continued: "We have found that the five senses do not testify regarding a reality, now let us see if they testify regarding an unreality. As we had agreed that death was the opposite of life and that life was real and death unreal, we will take death as our example. When a person dies, we say life, or the reality has flown, and the unreality, the material or dead body, remains. Do our five material senses testify anything regarding this unreality or dead body? Yes, all five of them, for we can see this unreality with the eye. If we move this unreality, we hear it move with the ear. If we reach forth our hand we can touch it. After decomposition sets in, we can smell it; and if we would put a piece of it into our mouth, as we do of the dead cow or bird, we could even taste this unreality. This ought to convince us of the unreliability of the knowledge transmitted to us by the five senses; for, as I have shown, they all say the unreal is real and that the real is unreal. St. Paul said, 'To be carnally minded is death, and to be spiritually minded is life eternal.'"

William W. Walter

"I know that St. Paul said this, but do not see as it has any bearing on the question we are discussing," said the pastor. "On the contrary, father, I think it is a verification of what I have been illustrating."

"Can you explain what you mean, Walter, so your mother and I will understand?"

"To me it seems plain, the carnal mind is the fleshly mind, which thinks everything is material; and this method of thinking leads to the belief in a material body and eventually in the death, or unreality, of this material body, the returning of the fleshly body to its original state, dust to dust, the real meaning of which I think is, nothing you were, to nothing you must return, for only the real is eternal."

"Walter, where do you get that definition of the word dust?"

"I take it from what is implied in the 2d chapter of Genesis, 7th verse, where it reads, '*And the Lord God formed man of the dust of the ground*'; as there is no record of any dust having been made, it is very easy to see that dust must be the name given to designate something that exists only in our imagination, a false sense of the real, an illusion, and this 'Lord God' the suppositional creator of material things, is the false or material sense of God entertained by us mortals, and only exists in our imagination. I believe our prayers are unanswered for this very reason that the God we have been praying to exists in our imagination only and is a man-made God, or, as I said before, a God conceived by man."

"Not so fast, Walter; let us finish one thing at a time.

Your explanation of the dust man is very reasonable, but I don't see where you get your authority for calling dust an unreality, or illusion."

"Father, I thought we had agreed that there was a hidden, or spiritual, meaning to all that was written in the Bible, and I think what I have said about this dust or material man is this meaning; take for instance, the first verse of chapter 3 of Genesis, which reads, *'Now the serpent was more subtle than any beast of the field, which the Lord God had made, and he said unto the woman, yea, hath God said ye shall not eat of every tree of the garden.'* Now, father, who ever heard of a talking snake. No one. It is only a myth, and I believe this snake was used to symbolize the narrator's idea of evil, tempting the children of God, Good, to do evil.

"Another illustration that this second narrative is metaphorically written is in Genesis 2, 9th verse, which reads: *'And out of the ground made the Lord God to grow every tree that is pleasant to the sight and good for food, the tree of life also in the midst of the garden and the tree of knowledge of good and evil.'* We can readily agree that there is no tree that bears fruit called good and evil, so this word 'tree' is used metaphorically, and stands for something quite different."

Here Walter stopped and looked at his father to see what effect his speech was having on him, also because he thought he had said enough for one time. But his father was leaning slightly forward and had been drinking in every word the boy was saying, as he was fully convinced that his son did not of himself know all these things about the Bible, and, consequently, it must be that he was inspired.

The mother had the same opinion, so did not care to interrupt him.

Walter continued looking from one to the other not knowing what to make of their silence and the knowing look which passed between them, as he did not know that they thought him inspired.

At length the father, said, "Walter, do you know what is meant by the word 'tree' in that verse?"

"I think I do, father; to me it stands for the word, 'thought,' for this seems to bring out the spiritual meaning of the verse; for instance, if we would read the verse this way, 'Every thought that is pleasant to the sight, i. e., understanding, and good for food, the thought of life also in the midst of the garden and the thought or belief in good and evil'; this may not be correct, but it at least makes it plain to me. And when we remember that Adam and Eve were allowed to eat of all the trees excepting this tree of knowledge of good and evil, it seems to me that they were forbidden to believe that both good and evil were real, in other words, to believe that both spirit and matter existed; for as soon as they would eat or believed in materiality the penalty would be death, as they were believing in something that did not in reality exist. This false belief must in the end inevitably result in death or annihilation, as it is this false belief of life as existent in matter, or material body, that dies and is annihilated, for the real or spiritual man cannot die."

"What do you mean by spiritual man?"

"The Bible says: 'God is omniscient, omnipresent,

omnipotent.' Let us define this word omniscient. In a common sense way, 'omni' means all, and 'scientia' means science, then it would be proper to say, 'God is all science, and science is perfect intelligence,' for the scientific reality concerning anything, is the perfect intelligence pertaining thereto. We can now say, 'God is all intelligence,' the word 'all' includes our intelligence, then God is the intelligence, the thinking ability, or mind, of man."

"Walter, do you wish to intimate that the brain is God?"

"No, father, the brain cannot think."

"Walter, this is nonsense, of course the brain thinks, we certainly do not think with our hands or feet."

"Just a moment, father, and we will see if the brain has the ability to think. Supposing we take it out and lay it on a platter, does it think?" "Certainly not, it is not in its proper place," said his father.

"It seems to me, that if the brain had the ability in itself to think, it could do so no matter what place it occupied."

"No, Walter, that would not be a fair illustration."

"All right father, we will now take another example. Say a man should drop dead on the street from apoplexy; there lies his material body, his brain occupies its accustomed place, not having been disturbed at all, yet you would not say that his brain had the ability to think?"

William W. Walter

"But the man was dead, life had flown," said Mr. Williams.

"Then it is Life that has in itself the ability to think, for everything else is there, in its proper place, and what is the life of a man but his consciousness, his intelligence, his mind. Now we have arrived at the same point in our reasoning where we were before, that God is Mind, intelligence, the Life of man, and that brains cannot think. You see, father, the brain is also matter, the same as the rest of our material body, that is, dust, or as I explained before, nothing; an illusion, or false conception."

"Do you mean to say I have no body at all?"

"No, father, what I mean is that man has taken a false view of his body by thinking it material when in reality it is spiritual, as is all the rest of the universe; for God, Spirit could not make a material world, as matter is the opposite of spirit."

The Rev. Mr. Williams leaned his head on his hand and was thinking deeply. Could Walter's explanation be the truth? He could see when what we called death occurred the consciousness, intelligence, or what we called life, seemed to leave the body and thereafter the body was inanimate, and in time returned to dust. Reasoning from this standpoint, he could agree that life and intelligence were the same, and that the intelligence of man was his mind was also plain, but that Mind was God, was beyond his comprehension, because he had always conceived of mind and brain as being the same, consequently, that the brain had the power of thought. Yet Walter's explanation concerning the inability of the brain, in the corpse, to think, and that it was as material as the rest of the body was quite convincing that brain, in itself, did not contain the power of thought. Was the boy right regarding the word omniscient? If so, it would be very easy to agree with him when he said that God was the intelligence or mind of man; he, himself, believed in an all intelligent creator.

Walter all this while had been waiting for his father or mother to express themselves, as they did not, he said: "If we can agree that Mind is God, then it is very easy to conceive of man as the image and likeness of God, and this image would be spiritual and not material."

His father looked up at him but did not speak. His mother said: "How would that help it, Walter?"

"If we reason from the standpoint that Mind is the creative force or first cause, and as we know that like produces like, it would be impossible for the creative force, or Mind, to produce matter, for matter is the opposite of mind. Now let us see what Mind does create, - why thoughts or ideas and nothing else, so we see that man is a thought, or a number of them, or idea emanating from the one Mind or creative force and the idea or thought must be the image and likeness of the mind or intelligence that conceived it. This would give us a spiritual man, who in reality would be the image and likeness of the real God."

"Walter," said his father, "I cannot stand to hear any more to-night, I will not say that you are right or wrong, as I must have time to think, and the more I hear you say, the more in the dark I seem to be, besides it is getting quite late and it is time we were retiring."

William W. Walter

"I hope you are not angry for my presuming to explain the Bible as I see it, for I believe I am right; in fact, I have had proof sufficient to convince me that it cannot be otherwise."

"No Walter, I am not angry, but very badly mixed up in my reasoning because of the peculiar views you entertain concerning God and man. What proof have you had that you are right?"

"Through these peculiar views as you call them, I am being restored to health; in fact, I believe every symptom has gone forever, and that I am entirely well, besides I feel so happy, contented, and free that I can hardly wait for the day when mother will understand, and be free from her bondage."

"If understanding will make her free I pray God that He will give her such understanding, but I cannot see what connection understanding can possibly have with sickness."

"You know, father, Jesus Christ said, 'Ye shall know the truth, and the truth shall make you free.' The question is, free from what? For the men He was speaking to answered Him saying: 'We be Abraham's seed and were never in bondage to any man, how sayest thou then, ye shall be free?' Jesus Christ answered them, 'Verily, verily I say unto you, whoso-ever commiteth sin, is the servant of sin.' At another time as related in Matthew 9:5, Jesus Christ intimated that sin and sickness were one and the same. He said to the *sick* man, 'Son, be of good cheer, thy *sins* are forgiven thee,' and certain of the scribes said, 'This man blasphemeth.' Jesus Christ, knowing what they were thinking and saying, said, 'Wherefore think ye evil in your hearts, for whither is easier to say, thy sins are forgiven thee or to say, arise and walk.' If we can now agree that sin and sickness are the same, we could say with Jesus Christ, 'Verily, verily I say unto you, whosoever commiteth (sickness) sin, is the servant of sickness,' for we certainly are the slaves of any sickness that we claim to have, and give it the power to rule us with a rod of iron, and in doing so, we sin against the first commandment, 'Thou shalt have no other Gods before me,' as we are making a God or power of our sickness. And if we take medicine, we are giving the medicine power to heal, or making a God of it, and in doing so we break the same commandment. Now, father, good-night, and I hope by a careful perusal of the Bible on this subject you will be able to agree with me. Good-night, mother."

"Good-night, Walter," said both his father and mother, as he turned to leave the room.

As soon as he was gone Mrs. Williams turned to the pastor and said: "To-night you must surely agree with me that the boy is inspired."

The pastor looked up at her and said, "That is the only way I can account for the wonderful things he says. I must admit he has gone far beyond me, in his understanding of the Bible. I intend to put in the next few days in verifying his explanations."

"James, do you think the boy can be right in regard to sickness and sin being the same?"

"There is hardly any other conclusion to arrive at, if we believe the words of Jesus Christ. Now let us go to bed, as it is quite late."

CHAPTER IX

THE CHRISTIAN SCIENCE JOURNAL

Bright and early the next morning Walter was up and reading in "Science and Health." After reading some little time, he heard his mother calling him to breakfast. He laid his book down and said: "This is the most wonderful book I ever read; no matter how many times I read it over, it seems like a new book, and sometimes I wonder if I had not skipped some of it when I read it before, as there are many things I see in it now that I did not see before. I suppose it is because I did not understand it all the first time."

Shortly after breakfast, his mother asked Walter to do an errand for her down town. On the way he began to wonder if Christian Scientists had a church or meeting-place, he also wished he knew of some one who was a Scientist, as he desired very much to ask some questions, particularly in regard to his mother's illness.

On his return from town, he was compelled to wait several moments at a railroad crossing near the depot, and as he stepped inside his eye caught sight of a little bracket nailed to the wall. In the bracket was a book, and on the cover in large print were the words, "Christian Science Journal." Walter hastily walked over to the wall, took the book, and began to examine it. He saw it was published monthly in Boston. Opening the book, he saw the first part was reading matter, and as he turned page after page, he came to where he saw, "List of organized churches of Christ, Scientist." Immediately he began looking if there was a church in his town. He noticed that the names of the towns and cities were arranged alphabetically. After searching for a moment he said, "Yes, here it is, 'Mapelton, Vermont. First church of Christ, Scientist, First Reader, John J. Sivad; Services 10:45 A. M., Sunday School 12 M., Wednesday 7:45 P. M., Number 52 Squirrel Ave., on Island. Reading-room same address, 2 to 4 P. M.' Why, that is only five or six blocks from my home; I wish I could go to their service. I may some day. They seem to have a great many churches; there are eight in Chicago alone; three in Cleveland, Ohio; three in Kansas City; three in London, England; six in New York City; two in New Orleans, La.; three in Portland; one in Paris, France; one in Melbourne, Victoria, Australia. "Why, they seem to be in every city in the world." He continued to read and turned the pages until he came to a page where he saw printed, "Addresses of Christian Science Practitioners." "I wonder what they mean by practitioner; it must mean those who practice Christian Science, but I should think every Christian Scientist would practice what he knows. I wonder if there are any in Mapelton; let me see, they are all classified in states and cities; yes, there is Mapelton. There are three of them here.

"Mrs. F. S. White, C. S., 281 N. Grant St.

"Mrs. M. J. Sivad, C. S., 742 Upland Court.

"Mrs. L. S. Poor, C. S., 45 Napoleon Ave.

William W. Walter

"I wonder if all practitioners are women; no, here is Mr. Sherman Bradford; here is another man; Oh, yes, there are a good many men, but there are more women than men. I know Mrs. White; her husband used to keep a shoe store, and Mrs. M. J. Sivad is that lovely lady who lives in a beautiful large mansion in Upland Court, the finest street in town; her husband is a retired merchant. And Mrs. L. S. Poor is that tall, stately looking lady that passes by our house so often. I must have a talk with them some time. Now I must hurry home or mother will think something has happened."

Arriving home, he told his mother he had stopped at the depot, and that this was the reason of his delay.

Walter was now so well and strong that his parents did not worry much about him, but Walter and his father were quite alarmed at Mrs. William's condition, for she had been failing rapidly for the last month and was so weak that it was almost impossible for her to do her accustomed work. Walter and his father did all they could to help her and made her work as light as possible.

It was several days later when his mother felt so ill that she could not get up at all, and so Walter decided to go to one of the practitioners for advice, which he did that same afternoon.

He told the practitioner of his illness and of his finding "Science and Health" and that the reading and study of the book had cured him; also that his mother was sick, that he was a minister's son, and his father was very much opposed to Christian Science. He also told her of their Bible lessons and of the confusion of his father.

The practitioner told him that the word practitioner was used instead of doctor or healer and that this was her profession, healing the sick, and that she would be pleased to help him all she could, but that she had no right to treat his mother without her consent.

Walter assured her that it would be impossible to get either his father or mother's consent, for they refused to have him treated at one time when a friend had suggested it.

The practitioner then said, "Well, Mr. Williams, your work is before you. Truth has found you, and Truth will show you a way out of your seeming trouble. Trust God and never doubt His wisdom, for God, Good, works in a mysterious way His wonders to perform; you must hold in thought that everything will come to pass as you wish it, and if you can persuade your father to have a talk with me, let me know, and I will be pleased to come."

Thanking the practitioner for her advice, Walter left the house and started home. He was not fully satisfied with his visit; many of the questions he had asked the practitioner remained unanswered, as he supposed, for the practitioner always referred him to "Science and Health." In answer to one of his most important questions, she said, "'Science and Health,' page so and so, says thus - "and then she would quote something from the book, but he could see no connection between his question and the quotation. When he arrived home he decided to tell his father all and try to persuade him to have his mother treated by a Christian Science practitioner.

CHAPTER X

HUMANITY'S MISTAKE

The same evening Walter went into the library to see his father, and found him seated at his desk with his Bible open before him. As Walter seated himself near the desk, his father looked up and asked, "What is it, Walter?"

"I came to have a little talk with you, father."

"I am glad you did, as there are several questions I wanted to ask you, one of which is in regard to that saying of Jesus Christ - 'ye shall know the truth and the truth shall make you free'-you explained before but I did not catch your meaning."

"Let us use an illustration to show what is meant by that saying. For instance, supposing we had been taught from childhood that two times two are five, and every person on earth believed this to be right, we would all go through life making this mistake. There would be constant trouble all over the mathematical world because of it, and when we tried to rectify this trouble we would use this same mistake in trying to arrive at a true answer. At times we would deceive ourselves and believe we were right, only to find later on that we were in deeper trouble. And when we had children of our own, we would still teach them the same as we were taught that two times two are five, and the longer the world stood, the greater would become this mistake, as no one knew the truth that two times two were only four; yet all this time the principle of mathematics existed and was correct, but man knew it not. Now father, imagine how great and widespread this mistake would become in several thousands of years, and how hard it would be to convince the people of their mistake, especially the professor of mathematics who had devoted a lifetime to proving that this mistake was the truth. You can readily see it would be much easier for the child who had never learned or believed in the mistake to grasp this truth than the professor who believed that the mistake was correct. Supposing that while these conditions existed some one should discover the truth, that two times two are four, and would bring it before the world; would not the learned professor ridicule the idea and say two times two have been five since the beginning of the world, and for any one to say different is nonsense? Could you induce him to investigate? No; why? Because he thinks he knows all about it, and that it would be a waste of time to investigate what he supposes is nonsense. So it is with man. For thousands of years he has been taught that he has a material body and that this body is intelligent, and knows when it has a toe that aches or a stomach that is out of order, or an arm that it can not move, etc., throughout all the ills that flesh is heir to. And when man gets in trouble through this mistaken teaching, we try to correct the trouble by making the same mistake again; for it was through the belief that man has a material body and that matter is intelligent that all this trouble came about, and now we try to correct the trouble by using more matter in the guise of medicine.

William W. Walter

"If we had insisted on the professor of mathematics who was using the mistake of two times two are five in his work, to give us a correct answer every time, he would be compelled to say that it was an impossibility. If you were to ask why, he would say, because the principle of mathematics isn't correct; he could not say otherwise, as he did not know that the mistake had been made in teaching him that two times two are five. So it is with man, when he gets so deeply in trouble that he cannot see any way out he lays his trouble to God and blames his perfect Principle, when the truth is that the mistake is not with the Principle, but with his own false belief, brought about by his being taught a mistake."

Walter stopped and looked at his father, but he said nothing, so he continued, "And when man goes to the professor of Christianity, the minister, and asks why all this trouble and sickness has come upon him, the answer is the same as the professor of mathematics made, by saying it must be the will of God - thereby intimating that God was the author of his troubles; in other words, that the Principle of man must be wrong. Instead of showing him that God, who is all good, could not make evil, and consequently, he must be suffering through a false belief brought about by being taught a mistake. Now let us suppose that some one should discover that man was spiritual and had a spiritual body, that the entire universe was spiritual and matter did not exist only as a false belief; that God made everything good, consequently there could be no evil, and that evil existed only in belief. If the one who discovered this truth should try to convince the professor of Christianity, the minister, that God made only the good and the evil did not exist, the professor would say, thou blasphemest, God made everything - if he should advance the thought that man was wholly spiritual, the professor would ridicule him, and say you must be mistaken, my body is material. I can feel it, and every man's body has been so since the beginning of the world. If the discoverer insisted that everything was spiritual in reality, these learned professors would say the discoverer was insane, and then try to pass laws prohibiting the teaching of this truth. In olden times they did somewhat differently; the learned professors of that day crucified the demonstrator of this truth. It was Jesus Christ, and His students were called His disciples; later when they went forth to preach the Gospel, 'good spell,' (or truth), and heal the sick, they were called apostles. The rediscoverer of this Truth at the present time is Mary Baker G. Eddy, and her students are called Christian Scientists; and later, when they go forth to preach the Gospel or Truth, and heal the sick, they are called Christian Science Practitioners, and he who condemns her teachings condemns the Truth, the same as the scribes and pharisees condemned the teachings of Jesus Christ; and it is the understanding of this Truth that sets us free, as Jesus Christ said it would."

For several minutes the pastor did nothing but lean back in his chair and stare at his son; then he said, "Walter do you mean to tell me that you received all this information pertaining to the Bible from a Christian Scientist?"

"No, father, what I know of the Bible and the explanations I have been able to make regarding the sayings of Jesus Christ, together with what I have said about the real meaning of creation as narrated in Genesis, I have learned by careful study of the Christian Science text book, 'Science and Health,' with key to the scriptures, by Mary Baker G. Eddy, and by comparing the writings in this book with the Bible, I have become fully convinced that Christian Science, as explained in 'Science and Health' is the same Truth that Jesus Christ taught His disciples. Jesus Christ said, 'These signs shall follow them that believe, they shall lay hands on the sick and they shall recover,' etc. Christian Science practitioners are doing this, and the signs spoken of by Jesus Christ follow their work. As yet I have only learned a few of the simplest things pertaining to this science, but this little helped me much."

"But, Walter, how do we know that it is not the work of the evil one? or a trick of the devil to lead you astray? I am very much afraid that you did wrong in not asking me about this teaching before you filled your mind so full of it."

"Father, you surely must agree that the things I have explained to you regarding the Bible are true, or at least nearer right than the way you were taught; and if you will only study 'Science and Health' you will soon agree with me."

"Walter, I have had enough of this; you have heard me express my views regarding this heretical idea; now I must insist that you stop reading such nonsense at once, I will admit that some of your statements seemed very plausible, but there is no proof that they are true."

"Father, I must speak more on this subject even though you accuse me of disobedience. I have ample proof that Christian Science is true, and that the signs do follow their teachings. One proof is that it was through the understanding I gained by the study of 'Science and

Health' that I am well to-day."

"Oh, pshaw, the idea that reading a book could have healed you of consumption! I credited you with more intelligence than that."

"It was not the reading of the book that healed me, it was the understanding of the truth this book contains that showed me the way out of my troubles; for if I had not found and studied this book I would probably not be with you now."

"Did you say you found this book?"

"Yes, Thanksgiving day, between the church and our home. At first I was afraid to read it, and probably would not have read it if it had not been for an incident that happened on our last trip to the South."

"What incident was that? I don't believe I heard anything about it."

"One day as mother and I were walking along the street, a lady approached us, and among other things made the remark that she read 'Science and Health' every day, and the reading of the book had healed her of some severe disease. This lady did not look like a bad person, so I thought if the book had healed her, it might me, and the truth it contains has done so."

"You have certainly gained a great deal in health since Thanksgiving day, but may not this be the work of the devil to lead you astray?"

"Father do you think it a good thing that I am well?"

"What a question, why certainly I do."

"Did you ever hear of the devil doing a good thing?"

The pastor looked surprised, but answered, "No."

"Then why do you say that maybe my getting well is the work of the devil?" The pastor could not find a ready answer, after a moment he said, "As I said before, I don't want anything to do with Christian Science, be it good or bad, and it will please me if you will never mention it to me again."

"Oh, father, I must speak of it to you for - "

"Silence! I will hear no more of it."

"But father, listen to - "

"Walter, I forbid you to speak to me on the subject again."

"Father, I must speak!"

"Do you dare disobey me?"

"Yes! for my mother's life depends upon my speaking. Let me speak this once on this subject, and I will agree never to mention Christian Science to you again unless you wish it."

The pastor's anger had been rising, but when Walter said his mother's life depended on his speaking, every particle of color left his face, and the anger vanished at once. He looked at Walter and saw he was dreadfully in earnest, so he said, "Speak this once, I will hear you."

"Father it was through the reading of 'Science and Health' that I was healed of the dread disease that is even now threatening the life of my mother; and as soon as I was convinced of the truth of this teaching I called upon a practitioner, asking her for advice regarding my mother's illness and asked her to give mother treatment. I did this without your consent, as I knew how prejudiced you both were regarding this subject, but the practitioner kindly told me she would not treat mother without her consent. And I knew mother would never consent to take treatment if you were opposed to it, so I felt I must gain your consent first. The practitioner would be pleased to come and talk with you on this subject at any time."

"No doubt of it, but I will have nothing to do with Christian Science."

"Oh, father, don't say that; you must be even more prejudiced than I thought."

"Yes, I am prejudiced, against all such nonsense."

"Father, will nothing change your views?" said Walter rather coldly.

"No, nothing."

"Then father, forever hereafter, I will ascribe the death of my mother to your unreasoning prejudice against Christian Science, for the medical profession cannot cure her, but Christian Science can." As Walter finished speaking, he arose from his chair and left the room; he immediately proceeded to his own bed-chamber, as he felt he must be alone, for he was terribly hurt by his father's prejudice against something which he admitted he had never investigated.

Walter had always supposed that his father was very broad-minded, but in this instance he thought him very narrow, condemning something he knew nothing about, in fact could not be induced to investigate or try, even though his dearly beloved wife's life might be saved by a trial.

It was at least a half hour before Walter could calm himself enough to think clearly. Then like a flash he remembered one of the sayings of the practitioner when he had told her that he thought he would have trouble in persuading his father to try Christian Science. She said, "Truth has found you and Truth will lead you out of your trouble." He now bowed his head and said, "Oh, God, I had forgotten that thou art an ever-present help in time of trouble."

He then secured his "Science and Health" and after reading for some time he stopped and said: "Here is what I have been looking for." Then he slowly read, aloud, "God, Good, is not the creator of evil." Continuing to soliloquize he said, "Of course not, God is Good, and Good could not make evil. Then evil does not exist, for God made everything that was made. Is prejudice an evil?"

"Certainly; then it does not exist in reality, but only seems to exist, because of the false report of the material senses. Then my father cannot be prejudiced. This must be what the author of 'Science and Health' called 'error,' and when the truth is declared pertaining to any error, that error ceases to exist-for an error can only exist as long as we believe the error to be the truth. When we discover the truth respecting a lie, the lie is gone, for truth has taken its place; the truth is there all the time, but we cannot see the truth because we believe the lie.

"I see my error very plainly now. I believed my father was prejudiced, and this was an error; in other words I believed a lie to be the truth. The real truth is that God never made prejudice and it does not exist, so my father could not express it, but it only seemed so to me, just as my sickness seemed real to me until I discovered that God never made it, but I had to prove it to myself before I could believe, or understand it, and as rapidly as I understood the truth regarding the error of sickness, just in the same proportion did the sickness disappear and the truth or health appear. Health was there all the time, but I thought I was sick, and my believing what I thought made the unreal seem real to me. I see now what that practitioner meant when she said my work was before me. I have another demonstration to make, at least that is what I saw it called in that Christian Science Journal. It means that I must demonstrate the truth regarding the existence of prejudice. It is easy enough for me to say it does not exist or to believe God never made it, and this would be a step in the right direction; but to annul this error entirely, I must be able to prove to myself, its nonexistence; that means I must fully understand the nothingness of evil under the guise of prejudice, and realize the ever-presence of Good, for if God (Good) is ever present, prejudice, or evil, is never present; now I must get to work.

"I made my first demonstration with the help of the Bible and 'Science and Health,' and with their help I

William W. Walter

will make this one."

It was nearly midnight before he stopped his work. He was not afraid of his mother calling in to see him, as she had been unable to leave her bed for several days, his father had been compelled to hire a servant to do the housework, and she was coming in the morning.

The Rev. Williams did not retire until long after midnight; he also had the same evil to fight, for he had admitted that he was prejudiced and so his prejudice seemed real to him. When Walter had first quitted the room, the pastor thought of calling him back and giving him a severe reprimand; but as he thought of all the misery the boy had been through in these many years of sickness, he decided not to do it. He then began to think of all that Walter had said throughout the Bible lessons and his thoughts were as follows "I cannot help admitting that a great many things he said seemed nonsense at first, but after a careful research of the Bible I found them fully substantiated and to be the real meaning; besides some of his explanations are very plain and prove his assertions. To think he got his information out of the Christian Science text book 'Science and Health,' with key to the scriptures, which nearly every clergyman and professors of all kinds have been ridiculing for the last thirty-five or forty years! Was there really something to Christian Science? Of course not; if there had been, all these learned men who had investigated it would not have denounced it. But maybe they were like me, so prejudiced that they denounced it without investigating. I even preached a sermon opposing it, simply because some one else said it was heretical, and as like as not this person never investigated it any more than I did, but denounced it because some one spoke ill of it to him. Now that I think of it, it was not a very Christian-like act to preach a sermon condemning something I have never looked into. Maybe that is what is the matter with us all; it is the same as sentencing a man without a hearing. I believe I will investigate this thing a little. I'll go over and have a talk with Parson Jones; he is considered a very well educated and broad-minded man; perhaps Walter was right when he accused me of being unreasonable; it certainly cannot do any harm to investigate. If there is nothing in it, I can tell the boy so, and if there is, it would be wrong not to try it for my wife's illness. Let me see, what did Walter say about its not being the work of the devil? He said the devil, or evil, could not or would not do good. This seems reasonable, and it surely would be doing good to heal any one of sickness. The Bible says Jesus Christ went about doing good, and this good that is spoken of was healing the sick and preaching the gospel. Yes, I'll just go over to Parson Jones to-morrow morning and have a long talk with him on this subject; now I must go to bed."

CHAPTER XI

FALSE INVESTIGATION

The next morning about 9 o'clock the Rev. Williams put on his coat and hat and said, "Walter, I am going out calling and will probably be gone until lunch time."

Ten minutes later he was seated in an easy chair in Parson Jones's study. After a few commonplace remarks he said, "Rev. Jones, I came over here to ask your advice about something I do not seem able to satisfy myself on."

Rev. Jones was a short, fleshy man, with red hair and face; he was noted for being a well educated and well read man, also of being very short and sharp in his speech, always speaking directly to the point. So he said, "Well, what is it?"

"I came to ask you if you know anything about this new cult called Christian Science?"

"Nothing to it at all."

"My boy, Walter, claims to have been healed by reading the text book, 'Science and Health.'" "A book full of rubbish, heresy, and nonsense."

"The boy is well now, and you know he has always been sick since he was a child."

"Reading that book didn't heal him."

"Still he claims it did, he stopped taking medicine, began reading the book, and soon we saw he was improving."

"Rest assured it wasn't the book."

"He does not claim it was the book, but the truth the book contained that did the work."

"Nonsense! there is no truth in that book."

"How, then, can we account for his getting well?"

"Probably the after effect of the medicine, or else he only believed himself sick."

"That is just what he claims, that he was only sick in belief and not in reality."

"Just as I thought," said the Rev. Jones.

"What do you mean, Mr. Jones?"

"He is another one of those simple-minded fellows who believed they were sick, and then claim reading that book cured them," said Rev. Jones.

"But I employed the best physicians and specialists, and they all agreed that he had hereditary consumption and was incurable."

"Most of these physicians are numbskulls and quacks."

"Do you call Professor Chas. William Canterbury of the University of Canterbury a numbskull or quack?"

"Eh, no, of course not."

"He examined him thoroughly about a year ago and agreed with the diagnosis of the other physicians; furthermore he told me the boy could not live more than a year, and it was about this time that he began to fail very rapidly," said the Rev. Williams.

"When did he begin to mend?"

"It was just at the time when he was failing rapidly that he found a copy of 'Science and Health' on the street, and he claims that as soon as he began the reading of the book he began to get better."

"This must be the work of the devil; it never was the book. You had better be careful, Rev. Williams," said the Rev. Jones, with a startled look. "So I told the boy, and he asked me a question which I would like to ask you."

"What is it?"

"Do you consider it good that my boy is well, Rev. Jones?"

"Why certainly."

"Did you ever hear of the devil doing good?"

"No," said the Rev. Jones, with a shake of his head.

"Then how can you say his getting well is the work of the devil who never does anything good?"

Rev. Jones sat back in his chair with a jerk.

"Rev. Williams, do you intend to defend this heretical cult?"

"Certainly not. I merely gave you the answer my boy gave me."

"A very bright answer, when you think of it," said Rev. Jones, rather stiffly.

"Especially so, coming from one of those simple-minded fellows who only believed they were sick and then claimed that book healed them." It had nettled the Rev. Williams a little to hear his son called simple-minded, after the boy had shown that his knowledge of the deep things of the Bible surpassed his own, hence his reply.

"Well, all I've got to say is that there is nothing in Christian Science," said Mr. Jones, with a bored look on his face.

"Rev. Jones, I did not come here out of idle curiosity, for you well know my wife has been sick for years with tuberculosis, and has been gradually failing until at the present time she is confined to her bed, and our family physician doesn't think she will ever get up from it. My son claims that Christian Science has cured him and that it will cure his mother if I will consent to try it. I told him I would not, and he said forever hereafter he would blame my unreasonable prejudice for his mother's death, and knowing you to be a very well read man, I came to you for advice."

"I have given you my opinion of it."

"On what do you base your opinion?"

"On what I have heard and read about it."

"Did you ever investigate it thoroughly, Rev. Jones?"
"Thoroughly enough to convince myself of the fallacy of its teachings."

"Did you ever talk to one of those practitioners?"

"No. They are a lot of hair-brained women and know no more than the author of 'Science and Health,'" said the Rev. Jones with a contemptuous toss of his head.

"Did you ever read what they call their textbook, 'Science and Health?'"

"No, my time is too valuable to waste it on reading nonsense."

"How do you know it is nonsense?"

"I have heard enough of what it contains."

"Can you quote something, Mr. Jones?"

"Yes, here are some of the things printed in that book:

"There is no death. You haven't a body. Your stomach can't ache. There is no matter. Brains can't think. There is no sickness. There is no sin. There is no evil. All is good, Good is God, God is Mind, Mind is God, God is all." He stopped and looked at the Rev. Williams, then continued, "All what, I would like to know."

"Are you sure the book contains these things?" "Certainly, I have it from a man who bought a book."

"If the book contains such assertions, it certainly must be nonsense."

"Nonsense, I should say so. No one but a demented person would write such stuff."

"I am glad I came to see you about this thing, as I hardly knew what to say to Walter in reply to his accusations of being prejudiced."

"Oh, it's always well to investigate a new thing of this kind before you condemn it, at least that is what I did."

"But you say you never read the book yourself?"

"No, I never saw the book myself, but my friend Dr. Thompson has one."

"Do you know whether he has read it carefully?"

"No, he never read it through, he intended to, but when he saw such assertions as I quoted to you, he could see there was nothing in it."

"Why, certainly, of course. You must excuse me, Mr. Jones, for acting carefully in this matter, because of the condition of my wife." "I would do the same if I were in your place, but you can rest assured there is nothing in it."

William W. Walter

"I suppose not, yet I wish there was for my wife's sake."

"You wouldn't dare use it if there was, they would cast you from your church."

"But no one need know it, Rev. Jones."

"Do you think one of those female practitioners could keep such a good thing? They would be pleased beyond measure to be employed by a minister, and would scatter the news to the four winds of heaven."

"I hadn't thought of that; thank you, Mr. Jones, for pointing out to me the danger of employing one of those Christian Scientists. I also thank you for showing me the nonsense of thinking Christian Science could cure my wife of something that the best physicians pronounce incurable. I must be going now, as I wish to talk it all over with my son. Good day, Rev. Jones."

"Good bye, Rev. Williams, call again."

"I shall be pleased to."

The pastor wended his way home, well satisfied with himself. Walter could not now accuse him of being prejudiced, for he had given Christian Science an impartial investigation, besides he was congratulating himself that he had been wise enough to consult with a deep-thinking man like Parson Jones, before employing a practitioner, for that practitioner would have delighted in telling it to every person in his parish, and this would have resulted in the loss of his position. The parson felt he had had a narrow escape from a great trouble.

As soon as he arrived home he called Walter to the library and told him of his visit to Parson Jones, and also what Rev. Jones had said regarding Christian Science.

Walter was somewhat surprised at the news, but after a moment he said, "You say you have given Christian Science an impartial investigation?"

"Yes, Walter, I have; you see I was not as prejudiced as you thought. I talked for an hour with Parson Jones, and he convinced me that it was nothing but a lot of rubbish and nonsense."

"What does Parson Jones know about it?" "Why, Walter, Mr. Jones is considered the best educated man in our city."

"Best educated in what?"

"In every thing in general."

"Did Parson Jones ever study Christian Science under a qualified Christian Science teacher?"

"No, I think not."

"Did he ever study 'Science and Health,' the text-book of this science?"

"No, he considered it a waste of time."

"Did he ever read 'Science and Health'?"

"No."

"Did he ever see the book?"

"He said not."

"Then he certainly must be a very bright man to know what Christian Science is. For a man that can know all about a science of any kind without taking instructions, without studying, without reading, without seeing the text-book of that science, is certainly a remarkably wise man."

"But, Walter, he got his information in a different way."

"How was that, father?" "His friend Dr. Thompson bought a 'Science and Health' and told him all about it."

"Was Dr. Thompson ever taught Christian Science?"

"No, I guess not."

"Did he ever study or read 'Science and Health'?"

"He intended to read it, but when he saw such ridiculous assertions in it, he considered it folly to read it," said the pastor.

"Another one of those wise men that know all about a science without instruction, study, or reading."

"What do you mean, Walter?"

"Father, if Dr. Thompson had told you that he knew all about medicine by simply glancing into a medical book, would you believe him?"

"Certainly not!"

"And if he had found therein some quotations that he did not understand, would you think it strange?" said Walter.

"No."

"And if he should tell you that those quotations which he did not understand were rubbish and nonsense, would you consider him a good authority?"

"No, how could he be," replied the pastor.

"Then, why should you believe him in regard to Christian Science, when he confesses that he never studied or read the text book of this science?"

"But everybody says there is nothing to Christian Science," said the pastor.

"So did everybody say the earth was flat until it was proven round," replied Walter.

"That's the point exactly; none of our learned men have been able to prove that the claims of Christian Science are true," said the pastor quickly.

"That is because they do not go to those who can furnish the proof."

"Who can prove it, Walter?"

"Many thousands of those who were healed and the practitioners in particular."

"Parson Jones said they are a lot of hair-brained women."

"Does that make them so?" asked the boy. "No, yet he ought to know what he is talking about."

"Did Parson Jones ever have a talk with one of those hair-brained women, as he calls them?"

"No, I don't think he did, but he says he has investigated this cult sufficiently to know there is nothing in it," said the pastor, rather quietly.

"I suppose, father, he gave it what you call an impartial investigation, and probably went about it in the same way you did. You went to a man for advice on a subject he had never studied and who was so prejudiced he would not take the time to prove whether it was right or wrong, yet he professed to know all about it, and advised you to let it alone. Now, father, if you wanted advice pertaining to a foreign country, would you go to a man who had never been there, and hadn't even read about it, or would you go to some one who had lived there for many years?"

"I should certainly go to the man who had been there," said the pastor.

"Then when you want information regarding Christian Science, why don't you go to a Christian Scientist?" said his son. The pastor was silent for a moment, then said, "I see what you mean, Walter; my going to see Rev. Jones about Christian Science is like going to a blacksmith for information pertaining to surgery."

"Yes, father."

"I guess you are right, Walter. I believe I will go to see a practitioner, for if there is anything on this earth that can help your mother I will let nothing stand in the way of a trial of it."

"Oh! thank you, father, I will go now and see if this practitioner can come to see you."

"Who is this practitioner?"

"Mrs. White, who lives down on Grant St.; she promised to come any time I would ask her to."

When Walter said Mrs. White, the pastor recalled what Parson Jones said regarding these lady practitioners telling all his parishioners, and the possibility of his losing his position; this made him very much afraid, so he said:

"Wait a minute, Walter, let us talk this matter over a little before you go. Had you thought of the position it would place me in to have a Christian Science practitioner coming to our home every day? And most likely she would be delighted to tell all her friends that the Rev. Williams of the Park Row Church had been compelled to call her in to treat his wife."

"No, father, I do not think she would say a word about it."

"But some of my parishioners might see her coming here every day, and then I would be in danger of losing my position."

"Father, would you let your position stand in the way of saving mother's life?"

The pastor did not answer at once, but was thinking deeply; at length he looked up and said, "Walter, your persistence has won the day. I will at least have a talk with this practitioner; you may tell her to come this evening if she will, and I will talk with her."

"Oh, father, how happy you have made me. And I know you will change your opinion of this lady practitioner after a few minutes' talk with her, and I feel confident that through her my mother will be made well."

"I pray God it will be as you say."

Several minutes later Walter was on his way to the practitioner's. In due time he was back and told his father she had promised to come that evening at 7:30.

CHAPTER XII

A FAIR INVESTIGATION

Promptly at 7:30 the door-bell rang, and Walter went to the door to welcome the practitioner; he showed her into the parlor and called his father. After a formal introduction, the Rev. Williams asked both the practitioner and Walter into the library, the pastor being afraid he might have some callers that would know the practitioner, although he did not state his reason for going to the library.

After being comfortably seated, the pastor said, "Mrs. White, I think it only fair to you to state that I have always been very much prejudiced against Christian Science and would not even now have consented to have an interview with you if it had not been for the persistence of my son."

"Mr. Williams," said the lady, "I don't believe you could be any more prejudiced than I was, and I only consented to try it after every other means had failed to cure me, and as I was not made well after one week's treatment I became skeptical, and wanted to stop taking treatment. But my husband said, 'Let us give it a fair trial, as there is nothing else for you.' The fact is that nearly everybody is prejudiced against Christian Science, and yet none of those who are can give you a reasonable answer why they are, and as a rule know nothing at all about it. So it does not seem strange to me to find you in this frame of mind."

"I suppose my son has told you he found a 'Science and Health' and that he believes reading it has cured him."

"Yes, he told me, but you make a mistake when you say he believes reading the book cured him; he doesn't believe it, he knows it."

"Why do you say he knows it, Mrs. White?"

"Because if he did not know or understand the truth that 'Science and Health' contains, he would not now be well, for these are the signs following, spoken of by Jesus Christ."

"Excuse me, Mrs. White, but I don't seem to catch your meaning; what signs follow the reading of 'Science and Health'?" "Simply reading 'Science and Health' will not help us, although it is a step in the right direction. It is when we understand the truth contained therein that the signs follow. Jesus Christ said, 'These signs shall follow them that believe, they shall lay hands on the sick and they shall be healed, and if they drink any deadly thing, it shall not hurt them.' If we use the word 'understand', instead of 'believe', we get a clearer view of what Christ meant when he said, 'These signs shall follow them that *understand*.' And as the same truth that Jesus Christ taught is contained in this book, the understanding of it must be followed by the same signs."

"But I am not willing as yet to concede that this book

does contain the Christ Truth," said the pastor.

"Mr. Williams, when you were attending school, suppose the teacher had given you a mathematical problem to solve, and had said, 'You will find the rule by which this example can be worked on page 105, and the correct answer is 18.' You would have looked up the rule and started to work the example. If when you were done the answer you got was 18, you would know at once that you understood the rule, and had applied it correctly. Thereafter you would not merely believe that you knew the rule, but you would know that you understood it. So it is with the sick; take your son's case, for instance; he found a 'Science and Health,' began to read and study it; in it is printed the rule of health. After a little study he understood this rule. He then applied it correctly and got the answer, *health,* and this is sufficient proof to him that the scientific method of healing the sick as Jesus Christ did, is contained in this book, and no amount of argument to the contrary can ever convince him that it is not true, any more than it would have been possible to tell you that you did not understand the rule by which you solved your mathematical problem after you had secured the correct answer. Correct answers are the signs following, or proofs of understanding, of any science."

"Then it is not God that does the healing, but the correct application of a rule," said the pastor quickly.

"Oh, yes, it is God that heals the sick; for instance, when you were working the problem mentioned above, you found the rule on the page indicated by the teacher, but the rule did not do your problem, neither did the mere application of the rule do it, but it was your intelligence, or mind, that directed the correct application of the rule that solved the problem; so to Mind must be given the credit of the solution, for the rule could not do anything without Mind to direct the application. And so it is with the rule of health; it is in 'Science and Health,' but to be benefited thereby it must be correctly applied by the intelligence of man, which is his mind."

"But this statement contradicts your first statement."

"In what way, Mr. Williams?"

"In the first instance, you said it was God that did the healing, and now you say it is the intelligence of man, or mind."

"Mr. Williams, do you believe God is all intelligence?"

"Yes, certainly."

"Then He must be the intelligence of man, or his mind, otherwise God would not be *all* intelligence." The pastor sat perfectly still, fully absorbed with his own thoughts. Mrs. White waited a few moments, then continued: "What I have said in regard to applying the rule is in full accord with the teachings of Jesus Christ wherein He demonstrated the necessity of us working out our own salvation."

"Mrs. White, you say that God is the intelligence of man, or his mind."

"Yes, for God is *all* intelligence."

"You also say that God is good only."

"Yes, God is *all* Good."

"Then according to this theory that God is all intelligence, you must admit that He is also the bad or evil intelligence found in some men, and if this be true, you could hardly claim that He is all good, for one statement would contradict the other," slowly said the pastor.

"You have made a mistake in your reasoning, Mr. Williams. A bad intelligence is not intelligence, but a lack of intelligence, or non-intelligence; in other words, ignorance, and ignorance has no place in the realm of intelligence, for ignorance is evil, and intelligence is good," said the practitioner. "Your explanation sounds very reasonable, but I am not yet willing to agree with you; it may be because I do not fully understand," answered the pastor.

"I do not think it possible for man to fully comprehend any science in a few moments, and this science is the science of sciences."

"Am I to understand that evil and ignorance have no place in the universe; in other words, are not real?" asked the pastor.

"Yes, the good alone is real. It is only through ignorance of the truth that evil seems real, or has place or power."

"But we see evil all about us," said the pastor.

"This seems so, but it is only a misapprehension of the truth, for evil is not real, has no entity or principle, God (Good) never made it," said the practitioner.

William W. Walter

"But if it is not real, and God did not make it, where did it come from?" asked the pastor.

Mrs. White's face broadened into a smile, and then she said, "Mr. Williams, I think I will tell you a little story that I wrote to one of my patients who was suffering from a claim of indigestion. She insisted that evil was real, and offered up the evidence of her indigestion as proof thereof. This little story came to me as I was thinking of her case. It may enlighten you on the origin of evil as it did her. Now for the story."

CHAPTER XIII

THE UNREALITY OF EVIL

"Once upon a time long, long ago, there was a great and good king, who lived in a country where everything was good. He had thousands of subjects under him, and these subjects were all good. This was because the king was good and the people strove to be like him. But one day one of his people imagined she saw an evil thing or devil, and became greatly alarmed thereat. She hurried home and told her husband what she had seen, and he believed her story about this evil, or devil (that never had any existence, only in the imagination of this woman). And because of her great fear of it this woman kept thinking of this evil constantly, until at last it seemed very real to her, and after a time she imagined this evil, or devil, had entered her body and was stopping her stomach from digesting its food. She also told this to her husband, and he became afraid of this myth, and told his friends that an evil, or devil, had entered the body of his wife. His friends began to talk about this evil, or devil, wondering what it might be. At length, after discussing it for some time, they decided they didn't know what this evil was, but that it ought to be given a name, so called it indigestion, because it had stopped the woman's stomach from digesting her food. In this way this imaginary thing became real enough to have a

William W. Walter

name. After the people had given this evil, or devil, a name, they all began to make suggestions of how best to get rid of him. One suggested that a plate be made hot and applied to the stomach. This, he thought, would make it so uncomfortable for the devil that he would leave. Another suggested that the woman take a strong dose of peppermint and burn the devil; another suggested that they manipulate the stomach, i. e., pull and haul and pound it, hoping in this way to kill him; another said, let us attach an electric battery and shock the devil. Another said he believed that devils had an aversion for blue lights, and thought that if they would let a blue light shine on him, he would leave. Another said, give the woman a bath of mud, let her be covered all over with soft mud, and this will smother the devil. Still another suggested that the woman be sent away from home to another climate, he thinking the devil might not like the change, and so leave the woman. Hundreds of other suggestions were offered and tried, but none of them succeeded in driving this devil out of the woman. And now, after several thousands of years, the people are still offering advice to this woman, but with no better success. The simple reason why all these things did not succeed in driving out this evil, or devil, is that in reality there wasn't any devil to drive out, as it was only an imaginary thing and had no existence, only as an illusion in the mind of the woman. About 2,000 years ago, there lived a man who was intelligent enough to understand what the trouble was. He said that there were not any evils, or devils, and that God, or the Creative Principle, was *good only*, and that evil was a lie, or delusion, and proved His words by His works. This enraged the wise men of His time very much, for they had been teaching the people that evil was real, and that in many instances God put evil upon His children to make them good. These wise men were sore afraid that the people would believe what this good man was teaching and denounce their teaching. So they conspired together and had Him crucified, and still continued their teaching that evil was as real as good. About forty years ago, a woman, intelligent and good, became conscious of the unreality of evil, and after a careful study of the life of this man who was crucified, she discovered that all this good man had said and taught regarding the unreality of evil, was the truth. She wrote a book explaining this great fact, and said, 'If the people would study this book, they could prove for themselves that there weren't any evils, or devils.' As in the time of the good man that was crucified, so in her time, the wise men were teaching the people that evil was real, and as the teachings of this woman were contrary to their teachings, they became enraged; and if it had been customary to crucify people in her time, she would have been crucified. Since that book was written, many thousands of people who imagined they had evils or were possessed with devils, have, by reading and studying this book, discovered that all of the evils, or devils of the past and present were imaginary, and seemed real, because we feared them. This book also teaches that the *only* way to get rid of these imaginations, or false beliefs, is to use our God-given intelligence and reason rightly, and then we would discover the nothingness of these evils, or devils, and our fear of them would depart, likewise the evils, or devils, no matter under whatever name they might be masquerading, as it was only our ignorance of the true facts, coupled with our fear, that made them seem real. So with this woman, who imagined she saw an evil, or devil; if she had not feared it, she would have investigated and consequently have discovered its unreality."

William W. Walter

As Mrs. White finished her story, she looked at Walter, and by the way he nodded his head she was sure he had grasped the truth of her story. Then, glancing at the pastor, she said, "Mr. Williams, does that answer your question, as to the unreality and origin of evil?"

"Mrs. White," said the pastor nervously, "That story answers my questions so fully that I haven't any foundation to stand on, and as I have been preaching the reality of evil these many years I am at a loss to know what to say or do."

"Do not worry or get excited, Mr. Williams, Every person is more or less confused as his old idols and gods are destroyed, but fear not, for out of this destruction will rise an intelligent temple with God, Good, the ruler thereof."

"But I am at a loss what to do. I have discovered the fact that I was mistaught in regard to the reality of evil, and now I fear that all the rest of my teachings may be at fault and I cannot conscientiously preach what is false, as God knows I would not wilfully mislead my fellow-man. I am afraid I will be compelled to give up my position at once, and feel I am not fitted to do anything else." He then glanced at the practitioner and said, "Mrs. White, can you offer me any advice?"

"Yes, first of all, remember that there is room in God's kingdom for all His children. Second, remember that your real source of supply is not your church, but God; trust in Him fully, and your every need will be supplied. Third, I would advise you not to give up your position on the spur of the moment; take time to consider, study 'Science and Health,' and see if it is what you want. If it is, you can then send in your resignation. If not, no one need be the wiser that you have been studying the book."

"But I cannot conscientiously preach one thing and believe another."

"Then, Mr. Williams, I would suggest that you ask for a vacation for six months, as I understand from what your son told me, that it has been a long time since you have taken one, and by the time six months have passed you will know what is best for you to do.

"Mrs. White, I would be pleased to take your advice, but I haven't enough money to carry me for six months without a salary."

"God is your supply, trust Him fully," said Mrs. White.

"Father, have no fear, God is all good, all love, and I know He will not see us want, if we will only trust Him."

"Walter, my son, I will take your advice and trust it all to God." Then, after a moment, he looked at Mrs. White and said, "Now, Mrs. White, let us talk of my dear wife's illness; I suppose Walter told you she has been suffering from tuberculosis of the lungs for many years. Do you think she can be healed?"

"Mr. Williams, do you think an all-powerful God could heal her? For it is not myself that does the healing, but God."

"Yes, I know that God can heal her if He will."

"Have you ever asked Him to?"

William W. Walter

"Many hundreds of times have I asked, prayed, begged, and beseeched Him."

"What did you expect to accomplish by your begging and beseeching?"

"I do not understand what you mean, Mrs. White."

"Did you think you could influence a good and just God by your begging and beseeching, to be more than good and just?"

"Oh, I did not wish to influence God," said the pastor.

"Then what did you expect to accomplish by begging and beseeching?" As the pastor did not answer, Mrs. White continued:

"A good and just God could not be less than good and just, and if this be true, what could we expect to accomplish by begging and beseeching? Mr. Williams, the reason your prayers have not been answered, is that you don't know how to pray aright, besides you have been praying to a false god, an idol of your own making."

The pastor's back stiffened up perceptibly, as he said rather cooly, "Mrs. White, don't you think your accusations are a little unjust? You must remember I am an ordained minister."

"Mr. Williams, don't think I am alluding only to you; almost the whole human race has made the same mistake. I am free to confess that I did not know how to pray aright until after I had studied 'Science and Health.' If you will allow me, I will try to prove my assertions."

"Please proceed."

"Mr. Williams, when you pray, do you or do you not have a mental picture of your god in mind?"

"Yes, most generally I do." "Will you please describe this mental picture?" asked Mrs. White.

"When I close my eyes in prayer, I usually see the spirit of God as though He was appearing through the clouds," said the pastor.

"Does this spirit of God, as you call it, have a human face?"

"Yes, Mrs. White, a face that is radiant with goodness and love."

"Mr. Williams, don't you see that this is a god of your own making, an imaginary creature of your own mind?"

"I don't quite understand," said the pastor, somewhat confused.

"When you close your eyes to pray, you imagine you see the face of a man, appearing through the clouds. You know this is not real, but the face appears only in your imagination, and when your congregation close their eyes, they each have an imaginary picture of some kind before them, or else a void, and if you were to compare notes, you would find no two persons to have the same picture or idol. Are there so many gods as that? If not, which one of the congregation has the right one? The fact is, most people pray to a god of their own making, a man-made god, a thing that does not exist, except in their own imagination, and then wonder why their prayers are not answered. Have I proven my assertion, Mr. Williams?"

"Yes, Mrs. White, you have, but you have also robbed me of my God, and now I am entirely at a loss."

"Better no god at all than a false one," said Mrs. White.

"That may be true, Mrs. White, but you do not wish to intimate that there is no God?"

"Most assuredly not, have I not told you that God heals the sick, that God is Good, that God is Mind? If I have robbed you of your false god, I have done a good work, for then you are ready to seek the true God. I recommend that you carefully study 'Science and Health.' In it I found who and what the true God is. If you will read this book, in connection with the Bible, you will find that it will unlock the mysteries of the Bible, and you will come into possession of that peace that passeth all understanding." "I shall certainly do as you suggest, Mrs. White; for I have determined to find the true God."

"Now, Mr. Williams, do you wish me to give your wife treatment?"

"Yes, I have determined to give Christian Science a fair trial."

"As it is getting rather late, I will not see your wife to-night, but will treat her absently as soon as I get home. I would also suggest that you acquaint her with the fact that I will see her tomorrow evening."

"But I have not asked her whether she is willing to take science treatment," said the pastor.

"Father, that has all been arranged, as I have asked her; all that mother wanted was your sanction. Otherwise she would not take the treatment, and I had acquainted Mrs. White with the facts before she came."

"I am pleased to hear that your mother is willing to try these treatments, as we have tried everything else, and now this is our last and only hope."

"When it should have been your first; yet that is the way of mortals, they try everything else first and God last, nevertheless God is ever ready to help man when man turns to Him, no matter what has gone before," said the practitioner.

"Mrs. White, your words give me great hope, yet my wife's case seems hopeless."

"Mr. Williams, why should you think it strange that a good, and loving, and all-powerful Father should be ever ready to help His children?"

"I know not, unless it is because He did not answer my prayers, and this may have weakened my faith," meekly said the pastor.

"But you did not pray to an all-good, loving, and all-powerful God, or you would surely have been answered; you were praying to a false god, even one of your own making."

"Yes, I know now that there was something wrong, and I supposed it was because God did not wish to help; but you have shown me that the fault was not with God, but with myself."

"Well, Mr. Williams, I am glad that the light of understanding is coming to your consciousness, and now I must be going. I have no special directions to give you regarding your wife except that I don't want you or Walter to tell a single person that your wife is receiving Christian Science treatment, and you may rest assured that I shall not tell any one."

The pastor was very much relieved to hear Mrs. White say she would tell no one, and supposing she did not wish to jeopardize his position as minister, he said, "I thank you very much, Mrs. White, for being so solicitous of my position."

Mrs. White's answer rather surprised him. She said: "When I told you to tell no one, I did not have you or your position in thought, I was simply thinking of the welfare of your wife. Now good-night, and you may expect me at the same hour to-morrow evening."

The pastor and his son bade her a hearty goodnight, then returned to the library. As soon as they arrived there the pastor turned to his son and said, "Walter, what other reason could Mrs. White have in bidding us say nothing of the treatments, excepting my position?"

"Father, I do not fully understand why this is done, but I have heard that they request this in all cases. I think it is for the same reason that Jesus Christ told them He healed, to go and tell no man."

The pastor looked at his son and said, "It may be for the same reason, although both are a mystery to me, at any rate this disproves the assertion the Rev. Jones made in regard to these lady practitioners being pleased to tell their business to everybody. Why, any one could be healed by Christian Science and no one be the wiser. I wonder if this does not account for the mysterious recovery of Mr. Anderson. You remember the paper stated that he was given up by the physicians, and that he could not live more than twenty-four to thirty-six hours; then to the surprise of everybody he began to mend rapidly, and in six week's time no one would think that he ever had a sick day in his life. And ever since he has been attending to his business, and every time I meet him he seems running over with happiness, joy, and good health."

"Father, wasn't he supposed to be suffering from a very severe case of Blight's disease?"

"Yes, he had a consultation of three of our best physicians, and they pronounced it Bright's disease."

"If it really was Christian Science that healed him, I am sure it will heal mother."

"Yes, son, I think so too, I believe I will ask Mr. Anderson what healed him, for if it was Christian Science, it will give me more confidence."

"Now please bring me this science book you found, as I would like to see it."

"I will get it at once, father," said the delighted boy, for he felt sure that if his father ever started to read it, he would never leave it until he had discovered the great truth the book contained.

In a few moments he was back and handed the book to his father, who said, "Walter, I wish you would call in to see your mother and acquaint her with what has been done; then you had better retire, as I may spend some time with this book."

"All right, father. Good-night."

"Good-night, Walter," said the pastor, as he assumed an easy position in his large armchair.

Walter went to his mother's room and, finding her awake, told her all about the visit of the practitioner, and also some of the things she had said, and that she was coming to see her the next evening. He then bade her a cheerful good-night and retired to his own room, a very happy and well satisfied boy.

His father continued his reading until long after midnight, and as he closed the book he said aloud, "It truly is a wonderful book, but I cannot agree with all that it contains, although this may be because I do not fully understand." He then wended his way to his wife's bedchamber, and looking in, found her sleeping peacefully; then he murmured: "I must trust God fully, for no one else can help her."

CHAPTER XIV

THE DREAM

The next evening at the appointed hour Mrs. White made her appearance, and after a few casual remarks, requested to be taken to Mrs. Williams. The pastor introduced her to his wife.

The practitioner, after explaining her purpose in calling, kindly requested the pastor to leave the room as she wished to be alone with her patient.

As soon as the pastor had left the room, Mrs. White turned to her patient and said in a voice full of affection and love: "Be not afraid, Mrs. Williams, God is an ever-present help in time of trouble, therefore I bid you hope."

Some of the languid and discouraged look that had been on Mrs. Williams's face seemed to fade away as she said, "You bid me hope, when all the rest of the world and my physicians have told me my case is hopeless? Surely you do not believe I can be healed."

"Mrs. Williams, I not only believe, but I know you can be healed, for nothing is impossible to God, and from now on He is your physician. Do not think it is I that is going to heal you, but our heavenly Father. 'He doeth the work.'"

"If I could only believe," said the sick woman, with eyes full of tears.

"Mrs. Williams, you can at least say the same as the man in the Bible said when Jesus asked him if he believed He could heal him; he said: 'Oh, God, I believe, help thou mine unbelief.' And this is what I am going to do, I am going to help thine unbelief, that is, cast it out, and let Truth reign in your consciousness. To accomplish this you must be obedient; if you have any prejudice, cast it aside. The word prejudice means to prejudge, and very few people are wise enough to prejudge even the most simple things of life, and those who do, are wrong more times than they are right."

"What you say is true, and I don't want to be prejudiced about anything, but there has been so much said against Christian Science and it has been ridiculed so severely that I find it hard to have any faith in it, yet I am very willing to give it a trial."

"Mrs. Williams, what would you think of a judge or a jury that would convict a person solely on the evidence of witnesses who were opposed to the person on trial, and probably all of the testimony was of this type: ('I heard Mr. Smith say he heard the prisoner had done it')? in other words mere gossip; would you consider this justice? Yet that is just the kind of trial that all prejudiced people give Christian Science. If Christian Scientists point to the great mass of evidence in favor of this science, this evidence is ridiculed and denied, no matter how honest the person may be who gave the testimony."

"Your contention is true, Mrs. White, I did prejudge or sentence Christian Science on the testimony of its enemies."

"I am glad to hear you admit this, as it shows me that one obstacle to your recovery has been removed, and you will now give Christian Science an impartial hearing and a fair trial. And now before I give you a silent treatment, I wish to set your thoughts aright about God. You may have said that it is God's will that you are suffering, or that He had put this thing upon you as a punishment, either for something you, or some one else, had done. This is a terrible thing to do, to accuse your Maker, a God who is all good, all love, of such a contemptible act as this. No, Mrs. Williams, rest assured God never did such a thing. Let us see what the Bible says on this question. In the first place, it says God made everything good; do you believe that?"

The sick woman nodded her head.

"Next, it says, 'And God saw everything He had made and pronounced it *very good*'; it further states that God made everything that was made; do you believe this also?"

"Yes."

"You have heard it said that Christian Science claims that sin, disease, and death are not real, haven't you?" asked the practitioner.

"Yes."

"Now let us see if their claims are true. You agreed

that God made everything that was made and that it was good. Now then, can you in any possible way show me wherein this claim of sickness of yours is good? if not, then God did not make it, it cannot be real, and it does not exist."

"But, Mrs. White, I have suffered with it for years, and it certainly is real to me," said Mrs. Williams.

"Let me show you how real it is, and what is necessary to make it unreal to you. Suppose I lie down on that couch over there," she said, pointing to a couch at the further side of the room. "As I fall asleep, the things in the room gradually fade from my sight and consciousness, that is, they become unreal to me, in fact they have no existence for me for the time being, yet they are all there. After a little I begin to dream that I am getting ready to take a trip to Europe. I pack my trunk, telephone for the expressman to take it to the depot, I dress myself in my traveling suit, get into my carriage, and am driven to the depot. On the way down I see some of my friends. I bow to them, and as I get out of the carriage at the depot I find my husband and sister there, to bid me God speed on my journey. I realize that my husband came from his place of business, and my sister from a distant part of the city. We enter the depot chatting gaily. My husband goes to inquire about the train. He comes back and tells us it is ready, and we walk down a pair of stairs and out into the train shed. As we approach the train, my husband gets out my ticket, shows it to the porter, and he says, 'Second car to the rear.' As we reach the place indicated, my husband shows the ticket to another porter who is standing there. He examines it and says with a wave of his hand, 'Right in this car.' We enter, and find the number of my berth. My husband puts my traveling bag under the seat, and we all sit there talking for some time. We then hear the conductor's warning, 'All aboard.' My husband and sister both kiss me and hurriedly leave the car. A moment later I see them on the platform. I hear the bell on the engine ring, I feel the car move, and wave a last farewell to those on the platform as they pass from my sight. A little later I am out in the country. Then we dash through a village without stopping, and at length we arrive at New York. I take a carriage to be driven to the dock. On the way there the horse becomes frightened, runs away, tips the carriage over, throws me under a rapidly moving street car, which runs over both my feet. The ambulance is called. I am taken to the hospital. The pain is almost unbearable. The physician examines my injuries and says he will be compelled to amputate both my feet. This seems so terrible to me that the shock wakes me up. For a few moments after I awake, I still feel the pain and lie there trembling with fright, for the dream has been so real. Yet in reality I never left the couch, and everything in the room is there just as I left it when I went to sleep. It was all an illusion, and the only thing necessary to prove it to me was something or somebody to awaken me. So it is with man. God made him perfect and everything good, and all man needs to prove it to himself is to be awakened, that is, made acquainted with the true facts pertaining to life. This means man must understand the science of being; then his delusion regarding sin, disease, and death will be no more real than my trip to Europe with its accompanying pain and disasters."

"I see the force of your illustration, Mrs. White, but I am sure I am not dreaming." "But you are suffering from a delusion, and a delusion is a dream, and is no more real. If it had been possible for some one to tell me while I was on my dream trip, that it was a dream, I would have denied it, because it seemed real to me. So with you, this delusion seems so real you believe it to be a reality. Nevertheless the facts were that I was suffering from a delusion, and so are you. So let us deny that evil is real, and we will wake up to the truth, or understanding, that it is not real. Now I will give you your treatment."

CHAPTER XV

TRUTH BEING MANIFESTED

The treatment over, Mrs. White said a few more cheerful words to her patient and then called the pastor into the room, saying to him, it would be well if he would read from "Science and Health" to his wife whenever he found time, which he promised to do.

A few minutes later, Mrs. White was on her way home, and the pastor and his family were more hopeful than they had been for some time. Walter and his father discussed with Mrs. Williams the happenings of the evening, and it was quite late before they all retired for the night.

Mrs. White came regularly every evening for about a week, and as her patient began slowly to mend she came only every other evening. The Rev. Williams and also Walter read to the sick woman every day, and by the end of the month Mrs. Williams began to stay up several hours each day. She also was an eager reader and student of "Science and Health." Many were the pleasant evenings spent by them in explanation and discussion of what they were reading.

True to his word, the pastor decided to trust in God for his supply, and had asked for a vacation, which was granted him. Near the end of the second week a letter came; in it was a check from a man whom he had loaned some money to, a long time before. It also contained a note explaining that he had always intended to pay the debt, but not until recently had his financial circumstances permitted it. When the pastor saw it, he said, "Surely this is in return for my trust in God, for I long ago reckoned this money as lost."

At the end of three months, Mrs. Williams was so far recovered that she was able to take care of her household duties and the pastor's understanding of "Science and Health" had increased to such an extent that he felt sure it contained the Christ Truth, but he was not yet ready to say he would give up his position as pastor. Walter grasped the truth more rapidly than his father, and whenever he found him perplexed or doubtful he was ever ready to point the way. His mother was constantly gaining both in health and understanding, and when Spring came and the end of the pastor's six months' vacation drew nigh, she was entirely healed.

It was at this time the pastor told his wife and son that he had determined to hand in his resignation and leave the ministry. They agreed with him that he could not consistently preach the old belief after understanding the truth; and as his congregation was very well satisfied with the minister who was filling his place, they would not miss him much.

A few days later he handed in his resignation. It was somewhat of a surprise to the directors, and they asked him to reconsider; but when he assured them it was final, they in due time accepted it and requested that he preach a farewell sermon. At first the pastor thought of declining, but did not; instead, he told them he would consider for a few days.

That evening, as they were all sitting in the library, he told his wife and son of their request, and said he had not fully made up his mind what was best to do. At this point Walter spoke up and said, with a smile on his face: "Father, do you remember one evening when we were having our Bible lessons you promised to preach a sermon on creation?"

"Yes, son, I remember."

"Why not preach that sermon as a farewell, for I know you can do so now with understanding."

The father looked at his son, smiled, and said: "Not a bad idea; what do you think of it, wife?"

"I think it would be grand and might be the means of showing some poor sufferer the truth. How thankful I am for this truth, and how I wish the whole world would know the Christ Truth."

"Then it is settled, I will tell the directors of my decision in the morning;" which he did, also telling them on what subject he would preach.

CHAPTER XVI

THE FAREWELL SERMON

The appointed Sunday dawned clear and balmy, and by the time the services commenced, the church was filled to its full capacity, the new minister officiating; and when it came time for the sermon, he announced that the Rev. Williams would preach his farewell sermon, and that the subject would be "Creation." The pastor slowly arose from the seat he had been occupying and leisurely walked up to and into the pulpit. He slowly allowed his gaze to roam over the crowded church, then began his sermon in a clear, full voice:

"My dearly beloved brethren, once again, after more than six months' vacation, I stand before you for the last time as pastor. I have been in your midst for more than fifteen years, trying to point out to you, to the best of my ability, the way to salvation. In that time I have made many staunch friends - friends to be proud of, friends that were true, friends that were friends in time of storm as well as sunshine, friends that have stood the test of time, and I hope will stand the test to the end of time, for a severe test of their love and friendship for me and mine is coming."

By this time every eye was fastened on him, and each individual ear was strained to catch his every word.

The Rev. Williams now opened the Bible he had carried to the pulpit with him, and said:

"As has been announced by your pastor, the subject of my sermon is 'The Creation.' In explanation I might say that just before, and during the time of my vacation, I was carefully studying the Bible relative to this subject, and I discovered the fact that during all the time I was studying for the ministry, and these many years that I have been an ordained minister, I had not become acquainted with the true facts regarding the creation of man. It was the discovery of this, with many others I have since made, that compelled me to send in my resignation, and in my sermon to-day I shall endeavor to make plain my discovery. I say my discovery, although it was not mine originally, but another's whose illumined spiritual sense is as far above mine as the blue vaults of heaven are above the earth. I will now read to you verses from the first and second chapters of Genesis. No doubt, you are all more or less familiar with them. Genesis, Chapter I, 26th verse, reads: *'And God said, Let us make man in our image, after our likeness, and let them have dominion over the fish of the sea, and over the fowl of the air, and over the cattle, and over all the earth, and over every creeping thing that creepeth upon the earth.'* Chapter 1, 27th verse, reads: *'So God created man in his own image, in the image of God created He him; male and female created He them.'* Chapter 1, 31st verse, reads: *'And God saw everything that He had made, and behold, it was very good, and the evening and the morning were the 6th day.'* Chapter 2, 1st verse, reads: *'Thus the heavens and earth were finished, and all the hosts of them.'* Chapter 2, 6th verse, reads: *'But there went up a mist from the earth, and watered the whole face of the ground.'* Chapter 2,

7th verse, reads: *'And the Lord God formed man of the dust of the ground, and breathed into his nostrils the breath of life and man became a living soul.'"*

As he finished reading this verse, he laid the Bible down and said, "I now wish to call your attention to chapter I, 26th verse. Therein is stated that God made man in His image and likeness. Chapter I, 27th verse, reiterates this statement so as to more fully emphasize this great truth. We now come to the question of what is God. We all agree that God is Spirit. If this be true, then man must be spiritual and not material, else he would not be the image and likeness of God, Spirit. In chapter I, 31st verse, we read that *God saw everything He had made, and behold, it was very good.* Now I want to ask, is sin, disease, trouble, affliction, or death good? It has been said that under certain conditions sickness might be good. I also thought this at one time, but in no way can we conceive of sin as being good. Then God never made sin, neither did He make disease and death; then whence came they? Is there an evil power that creates these dreaded things? If we believe this, we will have two creators, or gods, which cannot be true. Let us see if the Bible will not throw some light on this seeming mystery. Chapter 2, 1st verse, reads: *'Thus the heavens and earth were finished and all the hosts of them.'* Now this is all of creation, God has finished His work, yet in the same chapter a little further along we read: *'But there went up a mist from the earth and watered the whole face of the ground.'* In the next verse we read: *'And the Lord God formed man of the dust of the ground and breathed into his nostrils the breath of life, and man became a living soul.'* But God had finished His work some time before, at least so it was stated in some of the preceding verses. Is there a second creation, or is this simply one of the contradictions spoken of by some of our Bible critics? We can not conceive of an all-knowing God having made a mistake when He created man spiritually in His image and likeness and then later making another man materially from dust.

"I wish to call your attention to the fact that the Bible does not state that this *dust man* is made in the image and likeness of God, in fact it does not state that he was made at all, it simply says: 'And the Lord God *formed* man of the dust of the ground.' Then this dust man at best was only *formed* and never made. Neither does it state that God had anything to do with the forming of this dust man, as it does of the spiritual man made in His image and likeness, but states the *Lord* God formed him.

"Nowhere in the first chapter of Genesis, which is the true or spiritual creation, does the Lord God create anything; it is only after that *mist* (spoken of in the 6th verse of chapter two) arose from the earth that the *Lord* God *formed* the dust or material man, or anything else. Then the mystery of this seeming second creator, the Lord God, and his creation or forming of this dust or material man and material world must lie within this *mist*, and it does; this mist that arose was simply a misapprehension that arose amongst the people, wherein they believed themselves to be *formed* of dust or materially, whereas in truth they were created spiritually. And this *Lord* God spoken of that formed the dust man is not the real creator, the true God, but is man himself, who, through his own false idea or belief, formed man of dust, in other words, by his misapprehension of his true nature, man thinks himself material, when, in reality, he is spiritual, and it is through this mistake that all this evil or materiality seems to exist. But it is no more real than the dust man, and gets its seeming reality in the same way through a delusion or misapprehension of the truth. The proof that evil is not real, does not exist, and was never made, is contained in the Bible. Genesis 1, 31st verse, is this proof; it reads: 'And God saw *everything* that He had made, and behold, it was very good, and the evening and the morning were the 6th day.' I wish you to note that this verse says *everything*; this includes *all*. Then everything that really exists is good, it cannot be otherwise. Our God, our Creator, could not make both good and evil, else He would not be perfect, for evil is an imperfection and an imperfection can have no principle, hence no reality. Evil has the same reality that a lie has. What becomes of a lie when the truth is declared? It ceases to exist; so with evil; it being unreal, it ceases to exist, when Good is declared.

"Now, Beloved, I will quote you the greatest command given to man by Jesus Christ: Thou shalt love the Lord thy God with all thy heart, and with all thy soul, and with all thy mind.' I will now give you my interpretation of this great commandment: Thou shalt love the *Good*, thy God, with all thy love, and with all thy intelligence, and with all thy thoughts. Oh, if we could only do this, there surely would be no evil. Do we obey this greatest command of our Master? No. For instead of loving God, we fear Him, and lay every evil that befalls us at His door. If there be a cyclone, a flood, a cloudburst, a railroad disaster, a conflagration, an earthquake, an epidemic, we say it is the will of God. Oftentimes we labor long and faithfully to accomplish a desired result, and just as we think we have success in our hands, we fail, and all our hopes and desires are destroyed; again we say, it is the will of God. If we see any of our brethren sick, we claim it to be the will of God. If we see the father of a family taken away, we bow our heads and say God's will be done. If we see a family of children left motherless, again we bow our heads and say God's will be done. If we see a beautiful infant snatched by death from the breast of it's heart-broken mother, we meekly bow again, and, with heart full of sorrow, say, it's the will of God. I tell you it is not the will of God, the will of Good. There is no good in it, hence not of God's making, but is the work of evil, or devil, in other words, the work of a delusion, the believing of a lie. And when we stand meekly by and see evil destroy our health, our hopes, our happiness, our homes, without a protest, we are abetting the devil in his work. The Bible says God gave man dominion over *all* the earth, so rise in the might of your intelligence, your Mind, and destroy this evil, this illusion, this lie, with the sword of truth, in Christ's name. God, Good, is with you in this work, and with Him for you, who can stand against you? Too long has man been robbed by evil in the name of good. Jesus Christ said: 'Ye shall know the truth, and the truth shall make you free.' This truth has been revealed and is in our midst; 'seek and ye shall find.' St. John, the most beloved disciple, said: 'God is Love.' Can you believe a father who is Love would destroy the hopes of His children, make them suffer through accident, sickness, and poverty, and after three score and ten years let them die, in other words, kill them? Even the lowest of earthly fathers would not do this. Jesus Christ said: The last enemy to overcome is death.' This surely does not mean that we must submit to death, but the opposite, or overcome death. Christ's bidding us to overcome death shows that death is an evil. Then all things that are allies of death, such as sickness, poverty, accidents and the like, must be overcome, and when we have overcome all these things there will be no death to overcome; therefore I bid you awake from this delusion, this dream of life in matter, to the truth of life in Mind, in God. Simply believing in God is not enough, you must know God. Again I say, awake and work out your own salvation, as St. Paul said you must; salvation, is not believing, but knowing. In the words of one of the prophets, *acquaint* thyself with God and be at peace. Search the Scriptures, they contain the truth of life. Use your reasoning power, and do your own thinking-for the kingdom of heaven is at hand. Christ is risen and is knocking at your door, let Him in, and He will show you the way out of trouble, sin, disease, and how to conquer death.

"Now, Beloved, in conclusion, I would like to call your attention to my family, as you all know my son Walter was a sufferer for years from a disease that materia medica says is incurable; you now see him in your midst, a well and strong young man. I had long ago come to the conclusion that it was the will of God that he was sick, but through his own realization of the great truth that God made only the good, he was healed - in a like manner his mother, my wife, was healed of the same dread disease by *one* who *knew* that the good only was real, and proved it by destroying this seeming evil, which to us is known as tuberculosis. My wife is also in your midst, hale and hearty, as proof of my statement. And as I have also acquired this under-standing of God, I cannot consistently preach the gospel in the old way, hence my resignation from this church and the ministry, and now I must echo the words of that great man, Martin Luther: 'Here I stand, I can do no otherwise, so help me God.' Amen."

A PARTING WORD

Nearly, all my life I was an inveterate reader of fiction, trying in this way to forget my troubles and pain, as many thousands of others are doing to-day. During all this time there was a book in existence the study of which would have banished all my misery, but I knew it not. It is with the hope that in this way I may reach a few of these thousands and get them interested enough so they will seek the truth in the way pointed out herein, that this work of fiction is put upon the market. "Seek and ye shall find," and when found, hold fast that which is true and you will come into that peace that passeth all understanding.

THE AUTHOR.

William W. Walter